Under Maui Skies

AND OTHER STORIES

I Lalo o Nā Lani o Maui
a me Nā Moʻolelo ʻē aʻe

Under Maui Skies

AND OTHER STORIES

I Lalo o Nā Lani o Maui
a me Nā Moʻolelo ʻē aʻe

WAYNE MONIZ

koa books

KIHEI, MAUI

Koa Books
P.O. Box 822
Kihei, Hawai'i 96753
www.koabooks.com

Printed in the United States of America
Distributed in Hawai'i by The Islander Group, www.booklineshawaii.com
Distributed in North America by SCB Distributors, www.scbdistributors.com
Published in association with Punawai Press
Inquiries to Wayne Moniz, Punawai Press, 1812 Nani Street, Wailuku, HI 96793
For more about the book and the author, visit www.undermauiskies.com

Publisher's Cataloging-in-Publication

Moniz, Wayne.
    Under Maui skies and other stories = I lalo o nā lani o Maui a me nā mo'olelo
'ē a'e / Wayne Moniz. -- Kihei, Hawai'i : Koa Books ; Wailuku, Hawai'i :
Punawai Press, c2009.
        p. ; cm.
        ISBN: 978-0-9821656-3-8 (pbk.)
        Includes glossary of Hawaiian words and locations.
        1. Hawaii--Fiction. 2. Maui (Hawaii)--Fiction. 3. Hawaiians--Fiction.
    4. Hawaii--Poetry. 5. Short stories. I. Title. II. Title: I lalo o nā lani o Maui a
    me nā mo'olelo 'ē a'e.

PS3563.O5249 U53 2009
813/.54--dc22   2009

1 2 3 4 5 6 7 8 9 / 12 11 10 09 08

CONTENTS

The Roselani
Ka Roselani
Dedicated to Margaret Texeira Moniz
~ 109 ~

The Night-Blooming Cereus
Ka Pānini o Ka Puna Hou
Dedicated to Mary Texeira Torres
~ 110 ~

The White Ginger of California
Ka ʻAwapuhi Keʻokeʻo o Kaleponi
Dedicated to Lucille Moniz Coelho
~ 111 ~

The Mango
Ka Manakō
Dedicated to Rusty Monix Biddix
~ 112 ~

The Bougainvillea
Ka Pukanawila
Dedicated to Marie Moniz Steeley
~ 113 ~

The Cherry Blossom
Ka Pua Keli
Dedicated to Pat Yanagi Moniz
~ 114 ~

MAHALO

Special thanks to Paulette and Joe Medeiros, Guy Steely, Aunty Margaret Duarte, Aunty Evelyn Heu, Miriam and Bob Chipp, Joe, Julie, and Helen Cecchi, Rodger and Georgia Bridgen, Dave Peyton, Chris Hart, Mike and Martha Kretzmer, and Gene and Shirley Parola, who gave extra to make this book a reality.

Thanks to Hawaiian language consultants Ki'ope Raymond, Kaheleonalani Dukelow, Penny Davis, and Kalehua Darneal.

The publication of this book could not have happened without the help of Arnie Kotler and Therese Fitzgerald of Koa Books; Mardee Melton and Miho Owada, Eric Woo Design, Inc.; and Charlotte Boteilho and Cheryl Kauha'apo for their technical assistance.

Gratitude to the following publications where these stories and poems first appeared:

Wailuku, 1957, in *Literary Breeze from Hawai'i,* National Writers Association, Honolulu Chapter, 2003.

Aloha 'Oe, E Ku'uipo, in *Maui Community College Literary Magazine,* 2006.

Under Maui Skies, in *Hawaii Weavers of Tales,* National Writers Association, Honolulu Chapter, 2008.

PRONOUNCING HAWAIIAN WORDS

The Hawaiian alphabet consists of twelve letters—five vowels and seven consonants. The vowels are pronounced similarly to Latin, Spanish, Italian, and Japanese, except the letter "e," which is pronounced like the e in get. Hawaiian consonants are similar to those in English, but have less aspiration. Under certain circumstances (after i and e, and optionally after a or as the initial letter), the letter w is pronounced as a soft v.

Generally, the accent of words is on the second-to-last syllable. The *ʻokina*, or glottal stop—it looks like a "left apostrophe" between certain vowels—is a quick stopping of the flow of air, causing each of the vowels to be enunciated separately. The *kahakō*, or macron—a line placed over a vowel—indicates that that syllable should held for approximately two beats, rather than one. When pronouncing certain diphthongs (ei, eu, oi, ou, ai, ae, ao, au), emphasize the first vowel, then roll into the second.

PREFACE

The Hawaiian archipelago, in the middle of the North Pacific Ocean equidistant between California and Tahiti, is one of the most beloved landmasses on the planet. Its mountains and valleys, the shades of blue found in the sky and uninterrupted ocean, the touch of wind meandering from the northeast all play their hand in shaping these magnificent, remote islands. The islands were formed by an erupting geological hot spot starting about 5,000,000 years ago. Plant and animal life found their way here by air and sea over the course of millennia, evolving into species of flightless birds and post-volcanic foliage found nowhere else on earth.

Gods and men are said to have arrived in ancient times, including Pele, creator of land and fire. One of their offspring, the demigod Māui, was the trickster who lifted the sky and roped the sun to allow days long enough for his mother to dry her *kapa,* and he caused so much trouble that he was banished. Nearly 2,000 years ago, settlers arrived by canoe from the Marquesas and Easter Island, and a second wave of settlers arrived from Tahiti, "The Land Beyond the Clouds," almost 1,000 years ago.

Each island has its own legends, history, and dialect. Maui, toward the southern tip of the island chain, ruled itself with extraordinary dignity until conquered by King Kamehameha the Great of Hawai'i Island early in the nineteenth century. That was just a few decades after Captain James Cook and his crew of English seamen, the first non-Polynesians to touch shore, brought with them weapons, disease, and a very different worldview.

The two centuries since "contact" have been a time of profound transition. Hawai'i became an independent, modern nation, recognized by Europe and Asia's great powers. Literacy per capita in this formerly oral culture rose to be highest in the world. The newly written language had been crafted and taught by missionaries, who also brought churches, Western education, and Calvinist mores, and bore offspring who eventually overthrew the Hawaiian nation and established an oligarchy, then a U.S. territory, and, half a century ago, a U.S. state.

——•—•——

I grew up in the 1940s and '50s on a very different Maui from today. Sugar was king, along with pineapples, pidgin, and local pride. Ancestors of both European settlers and plantation workers dominated the local politics. Workers from Japan, China, Portugal, the Philippines, and many other places shaped local culture. My ear heard the rhythmic cadence of Hawaiian pidgin, now recognized by linguists as a unique language.

I was raised in Wailuku, the county seat and part of the verdant valley floor between 5,000-foot Mauna Kahalewai (West Maui Mountains) and 10,000-foot Haleakalā (House of the Sun), the strip of land that gives the "Valley Isle" its nickname. When plantation life came to a halt in the 1960s and '70s, community leaders decided to pursue tourism and development to keep the cash economy alive, and today Maui, though still remarkably lush and sensual, has nearly reached the tipping-point in the direction of overdevelopment. Locations of great beauty of my boyhood have become timeshares and condos. Beach access and fishing rights, though still extensive, have become more limited. Magnificent streams have been diverted and are considerably less pristine.

I am a playwright. Most of my plays are set in Hawai'i. To write a local play requires exhaustive research as well as conversations with *kupuna*, the elders of our community. Two years ago, while recovering from an illness, I didn't have the mobility to research a new play. At the same time, I began wondering if I had the skills to write the Great American Novel. This self-doubt led to a smaller step—short-story writing. Writing a short story would require less research, allow me to rely on my imagination, and, at the same time, test my ability to write a novel.

I envisioned a book of seven short stories—seven being a magical number—all set on Maui, each in a different genre. As I worked on the stories, I realized that each also represented a different time period and location on the Valley Isle. As I researched the background for the stories, I became excited, eventually loving all of them as my own children, each with its unique value.

As is true for my plays, most of the stories are based on true-life personalities and actual events on Maui. A fiction writer can then take liberties to bring characters of former times back to life. In all of my plays, stories, poems, and lyrics, I write to express my love for the land and people of Hawaiʻi, to preserve the memory of a time that is slipping away, and to encourage action to protect Hawaiʻi's magnificent land and culture.

There's no need to read all seven stories in one sitting. When you are in the mood for a love story, read "The Cruel Sun." If you have a hankering for a murder mystery, read "Aloha, Sweetheart."

I have dedicated each story to nā kupuna who have assisted and inspired my work.

Following the stories are thirteen *kaona* and one previously published poem. Kaona is a redirected metaphor that describes a particular person's traits by means of, for example, a flower, a waterfall, a tree, a bay, or another natural phenomenon. Nothing human is mentioned. Traditionally, it would be recited directly in Hawaiian to the one to whom the *mele* was dedicated.

When I discovered kaona several years ago, I taught what I had garnered from the writings of Mary Kawena Pukui to my students, and a number of them went on to receive awards for their own kaona in state writing contests.

I dedicate *Under Maui Skies and Other Stories* to Virginia and David Sandell, who have always been supportive of my work. I also salute our Maui writers, and all Hawai'i authors.

Wayne Moniz
Wailuku, Maui
March 2009

Under Maui Skies
AND OTHER STORIES

I Lalo o Nā Lani o Maui a me Nā Moʻolelo ʻē aʻe

Under Maui Skies
I Lalo o Nā Lani o Maui

A thousand stars glistened in the heavens, the moon so strong it seemed to penetrate Haleakalā's lei of clouds that teased distant Kahoʻolawe. ʻUlupalakua Ranch's thousands of silent acres had lulled Ramón Acuna into a meditative state.

His contemplation of the summer skies was broken by snorting, scrunching sounds in the nearby shrubs. Normally, *pouwaiʻu* did not include staying overnight with the wild longhorns. But this beast—tied to the strongest *kiawe* around—hadn't exhausted his anger that morning and was still full of fire.

"*Calle la boca!*" Ramón shouted at the two orbs in the dark. The bull snorted back in defiance.

Ramón had decided to stay the night. The bulk of the herd was back at the ranch for branding. His wife was in Hilo with the relatives. So Ramon took the time to heal his gnarled hands. People thought he had arthritis, but his hands, like twisted kiawe, didn't hurt. They just looked distorted from pulling strands of rawhide to make the well-known *kaula ʻili* and bridles, an art he had learned from his father.

Ramón was a descendant of the *vaqueros* invited to this land by King Kamehameha III to train Hawaiians in the art of cattle ranching. The vaqueros were skilled cowboys, but they were *mestizos*, the lowest of classes in old Mexico. Moving to Hawaiʻi, they raised themselves to a respectable level, which is why Grandma Lum was able to marry Ramón's grandfather, Ventura Acuna. Once married, he did not have to return to the poverty and degradation of Monterey.

Like a true vaquero, Ramón pulled, from underneath his blanket, the black guitar he had dubbed *Makaleka,* after his mother. Too showy, some Mexicans would say, a caustic comment to remind him of the caste system his family came from. Tonight he'd sing of the surreal world of Maui: a land of daylight moons, purple Jacaranda muffling the Kula hillsides, and the fragrance of eucalyptus wafting through its groves.

As he was about to sing his song of solace, a thundering jolt shook the campsite. The belligerent longhorn snorted and stomped the ground, and the hollow lava tubes beneath his feet amplified the echoes. These tunnels were dangerous. Ramón recalled when Josie Manoa took a mean spill, horse and all, into one of their crevasses. Ramón knew the bull was clamoring for a different reason this time. Someone was coming. The third-generation vaquero heard jingling in the dark.

"Ramón!" a male voice called out.

He recognized the faceless voice. How did anyone know he was here? Only Chris at the ranch knew, and he'd gone home early, because Rosemary was sick.

"Ramón Acuna? It's me, Henry Saffrey!"

"Sheriff, what the hell you doing here?"

"I'm staying overnight at my brother's place in Makawao to see the parade for 'Ikuā Purdy. You heard, eh? The celebration's tomorrow."

"Ho, he must have done good in Cheyenne."

"Broke the world record. Ran that *pipi* down in fifty-six seconds. Get one big shindig for him in Makawao town tomorrow."

"*Auwē.* I don't think I can get back in time. I'll stop by the house when *pau hana* for congratulate him. So whatcha doing here, Sheriff?"

"Ramón, I need one favor."

"What is it?"

"You going to do your usual thing tomorrow?"

"Yeah."

"Go all the way down to Mākena for check the walls and fences, any strays?"

"Yeah. So?"

"So you can keep your eyes on Albert Devil when you down there?"

"Albert Devil? What, he spreading cheer again?"

"If you call illegal drugs, cheer."

"Sorry, Sheriff, but as soon as I check out the pens, I gotta go Kahului for pick up Dolores. She's over in Hilo. Plus I no like being *nīele* about good guys or rotten ones."

"I'll pick up Dolores for you, plus give you some *uku* for playing deputy."

Ramón was curious about the money. He needed to cover Dolores' $5 roundtrip ticket on the *S.S. Haleakalā*. Henry uttered, "Twenty-five dollars," and Ramón's interest was stirred. That was a lot. His daily wage was 50¢.

"Before I say yes, tell me so more?"

"No need change your schedule. Do the same thing you normally do, but keep your *maka* wide open."

"You beating around the bush, Henry."

"Okay, hea's the scoop. We spotted one Chinese vessel anchored off the other side of Kahoʻolawe. Albert Devil hired a couple of local boys to take their canoes out, dive thirty feet down, and untie bags of opium hanging underwater from ropes top-side. The boys don't know how much the bags worth. Then they sail the booty over to Albert at Keawakapu for *manini* wage. All you gotta do is follow Albert from one distance. He not going suspect your usual routine. We gotta send him back to San Quentin and put away the distributor, too."

Ramón was hesitant. Albert Devil had a mean streak and wouldn't be afraid to use his Winchester, even on his own mother. Ramón uttered a belabored, "Uh."

"Promise, all *pau* when you get back home, Ramón."

"Okay, okay, as long as you no make it a habit, Henry. After all, I only one cowboy."

He raised his hand. "Let's get it over with."

"Do you promise to uphold the laws of the Territory of Hawaiʻi?"

"I do."

"By the authority of the Territory of Hawaiʻi, I hereby deputize you."

"Amen!"

"Well, Ramón, I better get outta here. I'll see you tomorrow night when I bring Dolores home."

Sheriff Henry Saffrey mounted his horse and galloped back up the trail, fading from the flickering fire. From the moonlit path, he shouted back, *"Mahalo,* Ramón. The people of Maui are grateful to you."

Ramón belted back, "Tell me all about Purdy's party later. No have too much fun."

"Aloha pō, Ramón."

The mountain crickets had no human interference and commenced their chattering on Haleakalā's 10,000-foot face. Ramón grabbed the coffee pot from atop the coals, poured himself another cup, sipped, and plucked a lullaby from his guitar. He eventually succumbed to dreamland in a warm blanket as the orange embers alongside him slowly faded.

A honeycreeper from the uplands roused Ramón from his heavenly sleep. The sun had broken free from Māui's house. Ramón cupped his eyes to take in the panoramic view, one rarely seen anywhere else in the world. All the trappings of a cowboy surrounded him. It could have been Laramie or Tucson or San Antonio, but those cowboys never had a bird's eye view of the furled bandana of golden beaches along the shore of South Maui.

With his spyglass he could see three-foot combers breaking at Keawakapu. He also spotted Albert Devil's campsite on the beach. The local boys would be back soon. They'd left for the anchored ship just before dawn.

Ramón suddenly felt a new silence. The longhorn had "kill fight" in him, and Ramón decided to let him be. He would deal with him later, on the way back. He gathered up his gear, grabbed one of Dolores' buttermilk muffins, slopped on her equally famous guava jelly, and washed it down with a couple of swigs of water from his canteen.

The air was crisp, but Ramón knew how hot it would get within the hour. He mounted Pāoa, remembering how, at its birth, Mother Acuna had said he looked like a chocolate-covered stick, like the famous, powerful stick named Pāoa that had led her Pele-clan ancestors to Hawai'i. Pāoa lived up to his name in the years to come. More than any other horse, working or rodeo, he always stood his ground.

The dry trail down Kama'ole yearned for November rains. A dusty cloud followed Ramón all the way to the lower corrals. Afraid of facing Albert Devil, he trudged on, cutting through a forest of *pānini*. The site reminded him of paintings he'd seen of eight-foot cacti in the Sonora Desert.

By the time he reached the Kama'ole pens, Ramón had broken a small sweat. Everything looked okay. From behind one of the high gates, he heard a muffled moo. Turning the corner, he spotted the stray.

"What's the matter, pipi? They leave you behind?" It was a calf that had probably wandered off in the shrub during roundup. The *keiki* echoed a doleful sound.

"*A'ole pilikia*," said Ramón, as he collared the calf. "You going home with me."

As he started to move the animal to the main trail, Ramón saw a black specter in the distance. The figure seemed to emerge out of the wavering mirage formed by the suddenly searing sun. It was Albert Devil, dressed from head to toe in black, like the Grim Reaper warmed over—black hat, black Levis, black boots, black vest. Ramón had to chuckle at the villainous costume. Albert Devil always played it big—and black.

"Ramón Acuna?" Albert Devil yelled out.

"Who's that?" Ramón pretended.

"Come on, Acuna!"

"Is that you, Albert D…?" Ramón cut himself off before uttering Albert's satanic last name. "Long time no see. I thought you went Califrisco?"

"No play games with me, Acuna. I paid my dues at San Quentin. I went straight. I one legal businessman now."

Ramón almost choked on Albert's lie. He noticed two large flour sacks hanging from a Kihei Nightingale. The donkey was tethered to the back of Albert's black horse, Maka'u.

"Flour for sell to the Kula folks?" he lied again.

"Yeah, the supply boat came in at Mākena Landing. Was a real bargain … for a businessman."

Albert Devil pulled out his Winchester. He cocked it. "Okay, Acuna, spill it. You spying on me?"

Ramón had anticipated the question. "Why you saying that?"

"Oh, only coincidental you stay hea'?"

"Come on, Albert. You oughta know by now. This is my job. Plus you think I want to be here when all Upcountry's at Makawao celebrating Purdy's win?"

"Maybe you spying for the sheriff."

"About what?"

"Uh, maybe he believes that I still one crook." He slid his rifle back into its holder. "I'll see you back in Kula. Maybe I'll buy you a drink."

"Sorry, I gotta tow this little doggie and one longhorn pau pouwai'ū up to the Wahine Pilau area."

Albert Devil kicked Maka'u. The donkey followed, burdened with the sacks of "flour." Ramón could still see Albert Devil, but he would drop back, little by little, to give Albert the impression he wasn't interested. His plan was to put the two animals in a higher pen. Fortunately for the new deputy, Albert's horse picked up a stone in his shoe by Maile Gulch, and it took him half an hour to get it out. This gave Ramón time to guide Pāoa up on the south trail to the ridge around Kula. He'd be there ahead of Albert Devil. The Norfolk Pine grove above town would be good cover for Ramón.

Kula Town was usually pretty deserted except for a couple of *makule* guys who sat, chairs back, whittling sandalwood scissors or whistles. But today, the hamlet seemed even more vacant. Ramón had forgotten momentarily that everyone was in Makawao. The only place open was Joe Santos' Lanai, anticipating some post-celebratory drinks after the boys got back from Purdy's party.

The silence was broken by the jingling cacophony of Albert Devil's spurs, keys, and chains. He scanned the area suspiciously. Then he looked directly into the grove Acuna was using for cover. Ramón did his best imitation of a pine. Albert Devil relaxed in his saddle. With the dealer's back to him, Ramón took out his spyglass and followed Mr. Devil to his rendezvous. Ramón suspected that the man in black might be headed for Ah Pak's place.

Ah Pak had not been on Maui long, maybe two years. He didn't come with the cane people. Shortly after he arrived, he "burned" a couple of folks in Wailuku, the county seat, and had to hightail it up to Kula to get away from irate clients. In Kula, Ah Pak bought and sold anything that could be bought and sold, to cowboys and farmers—including Albert's "flour."

Ramón couldn't hear the conversation but imagined what was happening in the parts of the playlet he did not see.

Ah Pak bubbled with enthusiasm at the sight of Albert Devil.

"Oh, so good to see you, Mr. Albert. I hope everything go well."

"What you so damn cheery about?" blurted Albert Devil.

"Well, so happy you have no problems."

"I ran into Acuna on the trail, but, when I last saw him, he went stop for one water break with a longhorn and keiki in tow."

"That's his job. No problem."

"Good. You get the $5,000?"

"Yeah. Up in the ceiling. Safe. But we have time. Why rush? We go Santos' bar to celebrate—as the *haole* man says—collaboration."

Albert Devil growled back, "What collaboration? I no exist. You neva see me before. Got it?"

"Yes, boss," Ah Pak trembled.

"And no call me boss!"

"Yes, boss … I mean Mr. Devil. We go to bar now. Here. I put the bags up in the ceiling … for safekeeping."

Ah Pak dragged a stool over to the opening in the ceiling. He pulled down the money from its rice bag in the attic.

"See. No need count."

He showed him a sample handful of twenties.

"You gyp me, *Pākē*, you die. I'm taking my *barato*."

Albert Devil snatched the rice bag with the twenties from Ah Pak's hand and stuffed the contents into another empty flour bag. He grabbed a coffee cup from the sink, scooped out two cupfuls of opium and put them into a second empty bag, plopped that atop the moneybag, and fastened it.

"Here. Put it up there. I'll get it when we come back from Santos' bar."

Ramón watched the twosome walk down the street to Santos' bar without the sacks. The vaquero could see Mrs. Ah Pak washing down the front porch. After the men left, her cleaning frenzy moved into—the kitchen!

"*Lōlō* husband, leave stool in the middle of …"

She looked up at the trapdoor in the ceiling; it was ajar. Curious, she climbed up on the stool and groped about. She pulled down one of the bags of "flour," stuck her finger in it, and took a taste.

"Yuck!" Flour gone bad! Stupid husband. Wrong place to store flour—too hot, too much humid."

She pulled all the bags down. She thought of tossing them down the gulch, but her crafty thriftiness got the best of her. She'd walk down the road and sell them to Lizzie Gomes, known for her *pao duce* and *malasadas*. If Lizzie rejected the sour flour to make her sweet bread and sugar donuts, Mrs. Ah Pak was confident that she could at least wrangle $5 for these slightly used flour sacks.

Ramón watched, confused, as Mrs. Ah Pak struggled with the flour bags down to Lizzie's place. He could see them negotiating. Lizzie finally, reluctantly, pulled a $5 bill from her bosom. Mrs. Ah Pak, bill in hand, raced home, beaming. Lizzie headed for the pigpens and emerged a short time later, locked the front door, jumped on the buckboard, and headed to Makawao to make it in time for the social and dance.

The sun was setting as Ramón watched Mr. Ah Pak and Albert Devil swagger out of the tavern. As they approached Ah Pak's, Ramón could see Mrs. Ah Pak waving the $5 bill from the porch. The troubled twosome looked at each other in horror and raced toward the house. Then all hell broke loose. Expletives were hurled along with dishes and furniture. Mr. Ah Pak and Albert Devil almost tore the front door off as they exploded out onto the lawn. Like maniacs, they raced toward the Gomes' place. Mrs. Ah Pak trailed, begging, "No hit! No hurt! Aye eee!"

Ramón moved off the hill to the road below and followed the dealers. He positioned himself near the *mauka* pasture and shrouded himself in the guava thicket that ran along the barbed-wire fence. Albert was in a fury as he dashed toward the locked front door. He raced around the back of the house, where he spotted the bags draped over the pigpen fence. Then he went into shock. A trail of opium led away from the pens out to a grove of *'ōhi'a* trees, a tranquil setting for—Lizzie's outhouse! Albert Devil opened the door and shut it just as fast from the stench that singed his nostrils.

Mr. Ah Pak, frantically trying to separate the illegal powder from the barnyard dirt, looked up. Albert Devil had murder in his eyes. Ah Pak knew he had to run, and he did!

Ramón stepped out onto the road, turned in the opposite direction, and pretended that he'd just arrived. Pursuer and pursued whizzed past him, Albert's eyes so angry red and Ah Pak's eyes so scared white, they didn't even notice him.

With his work done and the money and drugs at the bottom of the Gomes' outhouse, Ramón galloped up the road. Dolores was home; the porch lantern lit to welcome him. Pāoa's snorting drew Dolores and Sheriff Saffrey out onto the porch.

"How was Hilo, honey?"

Ramón dismounted Pāoa, ran to the porch, and kissed his wife.

"Raining, as usual. The family says hello. The sheriff wants you to help him out. You guys talk and come inside when *pau*. My sister wen pack some *laulau* and *poi* for us eat tonight."

Sheriff Saffrey walked over to the railing, took out some tobacco and paper, and rolled a cigarette. A slight fog crept down the mountain.

"What you got for me, Ramón?"

"All I can say is everything's back to normal."

"Where's Albert Devil?"

"The last time I saw, he was chasing Ah Pak down the mountain."

"Let me guess. Ah Pak went stiff 'em?"

"His wife did."

"So where's the dope and the money?"

"At the bottom of Lizzie Gomes' outhouse."

"What? Ramón, your $25 is down there too!"

"Well, as they say, Sheriff, easy come, easy go. Nobody want that *kālā* anyway, Henry. It's dirty money."

And so Ramón told the sheriff the whole story of Albert Devil as the moon peeked over Haleakalā, the same moon that shines down on the just and unjust who live and die under Maui skies.

The Cave of Whispering Spirits

Ke Ana o Nā 'Uhane Hāwanawana

The demigod Māui had not held on to his rope that day. The sun was swallowed earlier than usual by the Lahaina sea, and there was no moon. The 'ohana beached their canoes at *Keone'ō'io* Bay—named after the schools of bonefish that covered its sandy depths—and prepared for their long journey up Haleakalā.

Most of the 'ohana who had made the trip to *Kamā'alaea* had already returned to their upland homes. Only six family members were returning late—father, mother, son, daughter, and the young couple in love. The couple's trudge to their family *hale,* close to *Pu'u Māhoe,* would take even longer. With the sun setting early and the moonless sky affirming the blackness of night, they had to guess where the obstacles were along the trail. Unless they exercised utmost care, they might stumble and bloody themselves.

The littlest girl, *Ua Kaula'ela'e o Honua'ula,* was the first to fall. Tired and increasingly irritated, she complained to her mother, "Why did we have to come back so late? The others left on time."

"Don't think about the others, my daughter. It was a privilege for us to honor *Ali'i Nui,* our great chief, *Kaka'alaneo.* We went to see him, and now we have returned and must continue to serve him and the gods. And besides, who will feed the chickens? They will die without water, and we won't have a fine meal to feed Pele."

Her son, *Kiakai*, offered a solution to overcome the darkness. "I'll grab some *niu* leaves and husks from tree next to the canoe and make a torch."

As he rushed back toward the shoreline, his mother, *Kiaʻipukanui*, called out, "You cannot light a torch without fire!"

"I am not called 'Flint' for nothing, Aunty," said *Paea*, the handsome male half of the infatuated couple. "I always carry it with me."

"Praise Pele and Maui!" proclaimed his uncle *ʻEleiʻo*.

Kiakai rushed in from the darkness. ʻEleiʻo was proud of his son's initiative. As the men created a torch, ʻEleiʻo bragged that his hale had been dedicated to Pele and that, when she returned, it would be hers. Normally, *Kalua*, Paea's partner-to-be, would not be jealous of a god, but a smattering of envy overcame her when Paea went on and on about what he would do for *Wahine Ahi*, as though she were his beloved.

The flint eventually struck and the makeshift torch was set ablaze. Ua Kaulaʻelaʻe o Honuaʻula gave a small, frightened scream. The child, named after the cloudless rain of the area of her birth, squeezed out, "*He maka!* I saw the face, the face of a woman in the fire."

Her father quieted her. "Ua, you are tired and see things that come to your mind in fire and clouds."

"But father ... "

ʻEleiʻo stopped her. "Let's go! We're all very tired."

They continued the vigorous walk uphill. Only the starlight cast larger-than-life images against *Honuaʻula's* dry, dusty landscape. Kiaʻipukanui put her hand on her daughter's shoulder—a sign that she believed Ua's vision was indeed the fiery face of the goddess the men kept talking about. The mystery put her into a silence.

The *walaʻau* continued in the dark with ʻEleiʻo trying to outdo Paea about his devotion to Pele. He went on and on about the many fattened chickens the goddess of fire would feast on when she finally paid them a visit. Kiakai had moved out ahead of the illumination from the torch and, when he reached what was usually one of the flattest points, he fell headlong to the ground.

His mother ran to his side. "Kiakai?! Are you hurt?"

She dusted him off, as he grunted, "No." Looking closely at the ground, Kalua blurted out his discovery. "You know, I thought I knew this trail, but I don't remember a gorge here."

Paea was about to confirm what looked like the kind of ground rips Wahine Ahi made when she was irritated, but the adults kept their mouths shut, out of fear.

"Some wild pigs must have dug up the trail," 'Elei'o stated with false conviction, to calm the keiki. "*E hele kākou!*" he commanded.

A dog barked in the distance. "*Keawanaku!*" Ua shouted. Their family four-legged guard whined in excitement at the return of his masters.

"Ua! Stop! Your voice will carry down the mountain and wake up the village!" Even the usually dormant chickens mumbled low cackles of welcome to the family of the compound.

"You are welcome to stay the night with us," offered Kia'i to the young lovers. "You have far to walk."

Paea declined, feeling that he had to continue up to 'Ulupalakua, so that early tomorrow he could pull fresh *kalo* for 'Elei'o and exchange it for his cousin's sweet potatoes.

"If I stay, you'll get your *'ulu* a day late." The children drooled at the thought of fresh breadfruit. 'Elei'o passed the torch on to Paea.

"Have a good sleep, brother and sister," called Kia'i. 'Elei'o and the children echoed their sentiments, as the torch and voices of the young couple faded into the distance, continuing on their way up to Pu'u Māhoe.

The *Kauholanuimāhu* 'ohana was pleased with their lives of service to the gods, their compound no different from many others along the south shore of Maui. The *ahupua'a* they shared responsibility for was in one of the driest parts of the island, but its starkness was also its beauty—above them the majestic Haleakalā, below a dozen dreamlike coves, and, in the distance, *Molokini* and *Kohemālamalama*. The family grew sweet potatoes and fished Keoneʻō ʻio Bay. The caretakers of the upland ahupuaʻa came down the slopes specifically to trade their moist kalo for ʻEleiʻo's treasures of the sea.

That thought reminded ʻEleiʻo of something, and he announced to the family, "I'm going up to the boundary to leave an offering. I'll grab a few potatoes in thanks for this memorable day."

ʻEleiʻo left with the offering gourd, headed to the shrine at the edge of his boundary. While he was gone, the family prepared to settle down for the night. The females lit the *kukui* and prepared the beds, while Kiakai refilled the water trough for the chickens. By the time ʻEleiʻo returned, everyone was gathered before the family shrine, waiting for the final supplications and thanks before they lay down their heads. This gave the man of the hale one last opportunity to praise his fattened hens that would be Pele's when she returned.

Several miles up the mountain, the young couple approached Kalua's family home. *"He hone, e ʻolu ʻolu ʻoe,"* Paea said, begging for a kiss before they reached the hale. He leaned forward and pressed his nose against hers.

"Now is not the time," she recoiled.

"The only eyes that watch us are those stars, and they are without tongues." As she gazed skyward, he tried to embrace her.

"Look, the kukui are still lit. Perhaps *makuakāne* and *mākuawahine* are still up," she implored.

"They always have the kukui lit for their beautiful daughter. Listen, they are, as always, snoring vigorously."

"Goodnight, Paea. *E hoʻomaikaʻi iā ʻoe.* This was a wonderful day. I love you."

"Hui hou aku," he called back, and became one with the inky black night.

As Paea approached the *ʻili*, his small plot of land, he noticed the flame of a kukui lamp shining through the *puka* of his hale. He approached it cautiously, thinking that perhaps an untouchable had come in while he was gone. He picked up a stone from the path, just in case.

"Aloha!?" he called out. No one responded. No one was there. He did notice, however, a cover of ash throughout the hale. He thought that a blustery wind had blown Pele's breath throughout the dwellings in the compound.

He lit another lamp, grabbed the kapa, and fluttered it to rid the hale of ash, then redid his bed. He swigged down a bowl of water, chanted his thanks and remembrances of his ancestors, and blew out the kukui.

In the dead of night, Keawanaku suddenly began to run in circles, howling and barking; the alarm was matched by the chickens frantically cackling. 'Eleiʻo sat up. Before he could yell to the dog to stop barking, the earth began to rumble. All were shaken from sleep. Ua cried out, *"Mākuahine!?* What's happening?" A few of the *ʻaha* lashes near the roof snapped.

'Eleiʻo ran through the compound alerting all: "Get outside the hale; the falling posts could cut us." Everyone rushed out into the cool evening air, the children shaking in fear.

"Pele is nearby," Kiaʻi flatly said, Ua and Kiakai holding on tautly to their mother's sleeping garment.

As suddenly as the shaking started, it stopped. A dead silence permeated the mountainside again.

Several miles away at Puʻu Māhoe, Paea believed he was in a lucid dream, the shaking seemed so real. A brush on the head by falling *pili* grass convinced him it *was* real. His lover, Kalua, came to mind first and, when the trembling ceased, he raced down the path to see if she was safe.

Kalua's family gathered outside the hale as Paea raced toward his woman's family home. They stood in the chilly night, each giving his version of the the shaker, all agreeing that Pele had been angered by someone and this was a warning. After calming Kalua, Paea returned uphill to his hale.

Meanwhile, farther down the mountain, 'Elei'o and his family came to the same conclusion as their mauka cousins. Still, he told them that the snapped lashes were not critical and would be restrapped at sunrise.

———•·——

Sunrise came too soon for the weary folks of the slope. Ua and Kiakai didn't even hear the crow of the *moa kāne*. Kia'i had to rouse the family from their sleep.

"Wipe the *makapiapia* from your eyes, *e keiki*," she demanded. Their tiny heads poked out from beneath the kapa. "Another busy day. You played at the Ali'i Nui's festivities. Now it's back to daily life."

The children woke to see their father retying the lashes that had snapped during the night.

"What did last night mean?" Ua questioned, the face of the woman in the fire still on her mind.

"Someone has angered Pele, perhaps as she passed through this side," he suggested.

"Pele lives at *Halema'uma'u*," Kiakai insisted, taking his father's side to dispel his sister's fear. "I don't think she will ever return to Maui. She has found her home," continued Kiakai.

"Is she angry with us?" she asked, curiously.

"How silly, daughter!" said 'Elei'o. "Why would Pele be angry with us? We have been fattening the chickens. They are all for her."

"Perhaps your son is right," Kia'i suggested. "Pele may never come. You are fattening your chickens for a day that will never happen.

We had to go with little food last year while the *moa momona* stared at our flat *ōpū.*"

"And when that family from *Kaupō* came through a moon ago, you refused to kill even one chicken to feed them," Ua reminded.

'Eleiʻo sternly reprimanded them. "The gods must be satisfied. We are their servants and follow their wills. Those were merely commoners from Kaupō. We exist to praise our gods. We must be ready when Pele comes. Enough talk. Let me finish these lashings, then gather our fishing gear and gourds and head down to Keoneʻōʻio Beach. We are down to our last container of water." He had lifted the cover and looked down into the hollowed log that served as their repository of the *wai*, especially vital in this driest part of the island.

Up at Puʻu Māhoe, Paea opened his eyes, hoping the early morning tremor hadn't really happened. He looked out the puka; a fallen stone wall in his dry kalo garden had toppled and crushed some of his mature plants.

Something else caught his attention. A woman was sitting in the shade of his well-known *ʻalaʻa* tree; the sap acclaimed the best by bird trappers.

"*Aloha iā ʻoe,*" he called.

"*A ʻoe,*" she called back.

"Can I help you?

He noticed she was a middle-aged woman who may have once been a raving beauty. Her hair was streaked in white, the lines of experience across her face, her *kīhei* ruddy. He also noticed that she was staring at his young body as he moved into the glare of the sun.

"My lover has not returned and I'm searching for him. Have you seen any travelers from Kauaʻi?" She spoke through her eyes, the color of embers. It had a hypnotic effect on him.

"Can I offer some food and drink to strengthen you for your journey in search of your lover?"

"I'm beginning to believe he will never return. Perhaps," she said, teasingly, "I can stay here with you. You are a beautiful young man. Any woman would want to live with you."

"I can't," he responded, "I ..."

"... have a lover?"

"No," he lied. He was now sure that the fractured earth and shaker of the previous night were somehow associated with this woman. But this wasn't Pele, he assured himself. Pele would come majestically as a beauty. This was, simply, a formerly attractive older woman, more likely a demon than the goddess he adored. Whoever she was, her piercing eyes frightened him, and he contrived an excuse to leave her.

"Stay," he said, grabbing a basket of sweet potatoes. "I'll trade these for some fresh fish for you from my 'ohana down the trail. Promise you won't leave until I return."

His intent, of course, was to race to Kalua to escape the ominous situation. Hopefully the woman would leave before he returned.

"Promise you won't leave?" he lied one last time and ran down the path to Kalua.

Pele had indeed come to Maui, and Paea, in his fear and insensitivity, had refused the very one to whom he had dedicated his land and hale. Didn't he realize the gods could do anything? They could even change their appearance. Wahine Ahi could not only appear however she wished, she could leap forward and back in time as well.

Sure enough, she appeared just outside the path leading to 'Elei'o's compound.

"Kiakai," 'Elei'o yelled, burdened with fishing implements, "Don't forget the gourds!"

"Empty gourds are easy to carry downhill, father!" he yelled back.

'Elei'o's woman, Kia'ipukanui, saw the stranger approach the grounds. "'Elei'o, we have a visitor. A woman is headed this way."

"We have no time to visit. Get her some food."

"Aloha kākou," called out the visitor. "You have some of the finest chickens I've seen since I arrived from *Hawai'i Nui*. They must be delicious."

'Elei'o quickly blurted back, "Not for human consumption; only for Pele when she returns."

"What if I tell you that she's already here?" the woman questioned.

"You've seen her?"

"I am she."

'Elei'o choked at the thought. This woman was claiming to be Pele. Her face was covered with warts, she hobbled from a bad leg and, as she got closer, 'Elei'o and Kia'i could smell her bad breath—the odor of *uahi 'awa*. Perhaps she was an untouchable from Puna, judging from the smell of bitter smoke, disgraced, and now living off of the aloha of Maui. They were silent in disbelief.

Hearing voices, Ua ceased her game of *pala'ie*. She turned the corner and saw the woman. Her eyes widened like *'opihi* shells; she screamed.

"What's the matter, daughter?" Ua ran back from where she came. Her mother followed, aware from birth that her daughter had special *mana,* a sensitivity to spiritual things.

"It's the face, mother, the one in the fire!" she whispered, trembling. Kia'i believed her, that if it wasn't Pele then it was certainly a being with power.

"Kia'i," 'Elei'o shouted, "get this woman some food and wai for her journey. We have to leave now. Promise to join us later at the beach."

"But, 'Elei'o," she said, returning, "we have nothing, having been away, except some very dry sweet potatoes and a few pieces of equally dry kalo. You know how we anticipate Paea's return from 'Ulupalakua for fresh upland food."

"You have at least twenty fat hens," urged the visitor, "I'm sure Pele would not mind that we eat just one. And I'll just have a little of that. Your family can enjoy the rest of it tonight."

"Yes, that's a good idea, ʻEleiʻo," Kiaʻi affirmed. "Let me kill and prepare only one chicken."

"Leave those chickens alone!" He grabbed the fishing gear. "We must leave now; come on, Kiakai." He offered the woman a formal slight bow and headed out to the trail, Kiakai following.

The old lady turned toward Kiaʻi and frightened her.

"I'll take your meager offering and eat it up at Puʻu Māhoe. I am waiting for my lover to return."

Kiaʻi yanked the last kī leaf from near the puka and wrapped it around the stale kalo and sweet potato morsels. She handed that and a small gourd of water to the stranger. The visitor moved on the path, issuing a barely audible "Aloha."

"Mākuahine," cried out the girl, "I'm scared."

Her mother was equally concerned but tried to distract the girl. "Enough, daughter. We must put in some time in the sweet potato patch so this kind of embarrassment will not happen again. Then we'll head down to the bay and combine ʻopihi picking with some swimming and help father bring back the gourds of spring water."

Within a thought, Pele returned to Paea's hale at Puʻu Māhoe, eagerly awaiting the love of the handsome man, especially after being humiliated by ʻEleiʻo and his family. Her anger mounted when she returned to an empty hale. But she would give him some time. She planted herself near the entrance with her eye on the path, and fumed.

Meanwhile, at Kalua's family compound, Paea shared with his lover the news of the odd visitation of the woman. At first, Kalua disregarded the story as silly.

"I'll stay with you a short time, and then we can head up the path to your hale. If she's still there, she'll see you and notice that you indeed have a lover." She tenderly touched his muscled ribs to comfort him.

Pele noticed the shade under the ʻālaʻa tree shifting. With each movement, her anger grew.

As Paea and Kalua made their way back to Puʻu Māhoe, hoping the woman had left, ʻEleiʻo and Kiakai reached Keoneʻōʻio Beach. This was a most spectacular bay. Like Mākena's other beaches, its silky sands stretched long and wide. The water was as clear and sparkling as a fresh mountain pool.

"Load the gourds onto the canoe." Kiakai placed the containers on the canoe and the two headed out a good stone's throw.

"Can I do one gourd, father?" the boy urged.

"The last one, son." ʻEleiʻo flipped himself over the side of the canoe.

Kiakai passed the gourd to his father upside down, the lid on its opening. ʻEleiʻo dived down several human lengths to the mouth of the cold, gushing underwater spring, forced the neck of the gourd over the puka of the rushing fresh water, slid on the cover, and surfaced. They'd continue the process until all the gourds were filled with the tasty *wai puna*.

Pele looked down seaward on the *Honuaʻula ahupuaʻa*, boiling. A red glow surrounded the house, the house a liar had ironically dedicated to her.

As Kalua and Paea approached the hale, they stopped dead in the path. Flames leaped to the sky. Pele stared at them. The woman's figure suddenly became *ʻā pele.* The ground shook and a fountain of fire spewed into the air. Kalua and Paea stopped. "We must run, Kalua. Pele is mad with my lies. We cannot stop her now. Run, Kalua!"

Kiaʻi and Ua felt a jolt. The mountain shook. Garden walls fell, the pili grass roof tumbled to the ground. Kiaʻi thought only of the safety of her husband and son.

"Ua, quick. I know now that you were right. It was Pele, and she is angry. We must run to ʻEleiʻo and Kiakai."

At the beach, Kiakai was filling the last gourd when the ground shook. He could feel it underwater. His heart pounded as he rose to the surface. When he emerged, he noticed his father staring up toward Haleakalā, fixated on fountains of fire that came from Puʻu Māhoe.

"Pele is here! She's the one to whom I denied the chickens." He began sobbing as he spoke. "Leave everything, Kiakai. We must go get mother and Ua. The fountains of fire are just above our hale!"

'Elei'o was named after one of the greatest runners of the area and had tried to preserve the good name of his ancestor by excelling in his swiftness, as a boy and as a young man. Now older, his skill would be put to the test.

"I'll race ahead of you, son," he yelled back, as he bound up the hill. Stay as close as you can!"

Meanwhile, Paea and Kalua raced downhill. They watched as Pele transformed back and forth from human figure to lava. She raced after them, filling the form of the terrain as she tried to grab them.

"Kalua, head for the *Ana Mūkī*!" Paea yelled in terror to his lover. "The Cave of Whispering Spirits might save us. We'll mount the roof of the cave to avoid Pele, who licks at our heels!"

The now-growing vent was clogged with large balls of matter. They squeezed and squeezed to exit, like a troublesome birth. Finally, with an explosion, the balls whistled high into the air, exploded, and pelted the direction in which the lovers ran. A sizeable ember fell on Paea's back. He screamed in pain and continued to run.

Like a rip along a kapa cloth, a vent opened at the same time at 'Elei'o's compound with such a shake that both Kia'i and Ua, running downhill, and 'Elei'o and Kiakai, running mauka, fell to the ground. Kia'i looked back and saw Pele in the fast-pouring fountain. Her arms surrounded the two females. They would try to break Pele's embrace by finding the weakest area of the flow and try, despite the possibility of severe burns, to make it beyond the grasp of the angry goddess. There was a small section Kia'i observed back uphill to the north. She grabbed Ua and headed in the direction back up closer to her house. Suddenly, she looked down in disgust as several dead chickens flowed by.

"How stupid we were!" she thought. But it was too late. The ground split open, and Ua and her mother were separated by a wide gap.

"Mother!" Ua cried out for help.

Kiaʻi felt as helpless as any mother could be.

"Run, *kuʻu ipo*, run!"

"There is no place to run, mother. ... " The girl formed a face of futility. At that moment, a thick spray of hot lava landed on both, molding them into *kiʻi* of *ʻaʻā* to the left and right of the gaping vent.

At the same time, Paea and Kalua reached the Cave of Whispering Spirits. As Paea climbed to the top to survey the area, a wave of lava separated him from Kalua. The wave lapped up against the cave. Paea spotted an area not touched by Pele's outreach.

"Kalua, to your left! Run, now, downhill!"

"I can't, Paea. I can't leave you. I love you."

"No time for further foolishness! Save your life!"

"No, Paea."

"You'll make me most happy if you would live life to its fullest. Go. Run and live!"

Kalua started to leave, then turned sadly to watch Pele grab her lover. The goddess of fire stretched him out the length of the flow, his head toward ʻUlupalakua, his feet toward the sea.

Kalua raced downhill in a narrow corridor of unscorched soil as Pele continued to stretch Paea toward the sea. She could see ʻEleiʻo's land area below her, now spewing a fountain. She heard, in her head, the voice of a scorned Pele.

"Now join your lover, Kalua."

Just as she reached *Puʻu Naio*, she stumbled. As Kalua tried to stand up, she heard hissing behind her. It was too late. As she looked up, a wall of lava overwhelmed her. Like her lover, her body was swept along, elongated in Pele's hot blood. She became part of two flows racing parallel down the mountain to Keoneʻōʻio Bay.

Simultaneously, ʻEleiʻo had been racing to high ground, Kiakai behind him. Saving his wife and daughter was becoming less likely, as ash and smoke obscured his forward progress. He longed to see them one more time. He had made the fatal mistake humans sometimes make—ignoring a god.

He would see his house shortly and, gratefully, Kiaʻipukanui and Ua Kaulaʻelaʻe o Honuaʻula. As he mounted the ridge, he stopped on the hill—a small dark figure against a blazing, blood-red sky. Kiakai finally caught up to him, and both stood staring in fright at the scene. Their compound was gone and, in its place, a gaping vent spewing the guts of Pele. He hugged his son, tears flowing from each of them. And there, on either side of the vent, he recognized the woman and daughter he loved, sentinels at the *piko* of Pele.

Suddenly, a large boom heralded a spray of stones from the vent. They splashed into the stream that was now beginning to surround them.

"Run ... back down ... toward the ocean, Kiakai!" he shouted.

At their heels fell a barrage of flaming hot *pōhaku*. Their years as hardy walkers and strong runners helped them dodge the falling stones.

ʻEleiʻo wanted to break *ʻākau* toward Mākena or *hema* toward Kanaio, but a wall ran beside them in both directions. The only choice was the sea. Never was Keoneʻōʻio Bay so welcome. The two fingers of lava trailed father and son all the way to the beach.

"Into the water, Kiakai. If we have to swim to Molokini, we will!" he screamed. As the two entered the surf, a volley of rocks cascaded down upon them like the war clubs of *nā koa*. The barrage of deadly stones pummelled father and son. As the last breaths of life moved from their bodies, ʻEleiʻo looked into the eyes of his son.

"I'm sorry, son ... to our family ... to Pele."

Their eyes closed almost simultaneously, their bodies dangling lifeless in the pristine water. The flows to the left and right merged and covered them, leaving two ʻaʻā-covered posts submerged some two body lengths below the surface.

————

On *Muku*, in future generations, when the moon is missing, soft, sad voices tell a tale, a tale of the foolishness of a family and young couple who, ironically, dedicated their whole lives to Pele but were unaware, because of their vanity, to recognize and care for her when at last she came. The tragedy of their metamorphosis by Wahine Ahi is heard by those who pass or enter Ana Mūkī, the Cave of Whispering Spirits.

The Cruel Sun
Ka Lā Hainā

Her leg was wrapped about his thigh; her hand skimmed smoothly over his chest. She could feel his heart beating as she had many times before. The moon beamed down and glistened their brown bodies, the admired, peaked physiques of youth. 'Īao Stream whispered approval a few feet away, just below a basalt bed carved naturally for two, frozen after the caldera had cooled. It was as though the gods had instigated this night. Harriet felt Kaui's heart suddenly race.

"What?" she responded.

Kaui turned over frustratingly to face the full moon.

"I just can't understand why they think that this pleasure is sinful."

"I know, Kaui."

"What could anyone want more than you, the sweet ginger fragrance in your hair, the peace you give me."

She felt the same way about him, and responded, "How ironic that they profess love but only love of the mind, abstract, not love in a world of bodies."

"Kauiiiiiii!" A voice echoed out from the shadows.

The two naked bodies grabbed for their *malo* hanging in the branches of a nearby *kuava* tree.

"It's Kina'u!" Harriet whispered.

"Child of Kā'u, where are you?" she bellowed.

"We're coming!" they yelled back in unison.

Kinaʻu emerged out of the darkness into the moonlight. She was huffing. "Ho … I had to walk … all this distance up the valley … Mr. Richards is on his … way and I knew you would not like to have him find you like this."

"To hell with Mr. Richards," Kaui retorted.

"You don't mean that, Kaui," said Kinaʻu.

Kaui countered with silence.

The awkwardness was broken by Harriet. "We want to get married."

Even Kaui was startled by her bluntness. He knew that if Kinaʻu were white and Christian, she would have protested vehemently, but, like Kaui, Kinaʻu's old ways were despondently clashing with the new. She tried another tact.

"Harriet, your mother would have frowned upon that, having converted in her last days. You wouldn't want to disappoint her, would you?"

A silence fell over the teen. Kinaʻu guiltily noticed the effect her words had on the girl.

"Come on. Let's get back before Mr. Richards arrives."

Kinaʻu turned and plodded ahead. She pretended not to notice the two holding hands behind her in the distance.

"E ʻawīwī. E ʻawīwī," she commanded every number of steps. Kaui whispered as they walked down the trail.

"After Richards has gone and the others are asleep, I'll take you to this pond a little ways beyond the camp. I have a pint of brandy."

They had barely washed and changed before Richards and two assistants arrived for dinner. Harriet's spiritual advisor was, in Kaui's words, continuously nīele as the couple encircled the island, meeting with the people from each community, copying the journeys of Paieʻa, the Great Kamehameha. Richards, the missionary, had even made the trip out to isolated Kaupō to make sure his young, female sire was on the spiritual straight and narrow.

Harriet put on her best face during her after-dinner counseling session, occasionally scrunching up her nose to Kaui when the "man of God" wasn't looking, Kinaʻu giving her stink eye as she prepared the couple's sleeping area.

After Richards' horses' hoofbeats faded in the distance, the retinue fell into a snoring state. When the embers of the campfire diminished, Kaui shook the wide-awake Harriet at the elbow, his hand cupped over her lips. Then, with the same hand, he led her along a trail of fallen kukui leaves. They leaped from boulder to boulder in the crisp moonlight.

"This is a place of lovers," he said to her softly. She looked quizzically at him. He continued, "This is the place where ʻĪao and Puʻuokamoa met secretly as we do now."

Of course, Harriet knew of the forbidden affair between the daughter of Maui and the merman of the stream.

"How do you know?" Kaui confessed.

"Well, actually I don't, but after we finish this brandy, hell, it could be where Napoleon met Désirée."

They found a soft, sand-like area. Kaui grabbed a clump of fragile *lauaʻe* growing beside a nearby eddy and, as she reclined, placed it as a pillow under his lover's head. Then he pulled the pint of liquor out from under his malo.

"You first, my queen."

"No, I insist, you first, my king." He jutted the bottle out to her. She giggled taking the first sip.

After they had consumed half the bottle, Richards' harsh world fell away. The sweetness of the brandy made Harriet's lips even sweeter. The boldness of the liquor intensified Kaui's boldness.

"We don't need permission from anyone to get married. It is our life," Kaui insisted.

She nodded in agreement and continued, "But I don't know if I'll be able to handle the protests, you know, from the Christian brethren."

"I guess they haven't heard that when visiting Hawai'i, one should do what the *kanaka maoli* do. These scoundrels aren't satisfied with stealing the *'āina*. They want to break our wills as well."

Harriet stroked his face, warmed now by the brandy. She sipped gently, but heartily.

"Perhaps it can be a ceremony done quietly. We don't have to get Kina'u into trouble. We'll keep it from her as well, and tell her afterwards."

Kaui lit up.

"Pākī would do it. He is of the old ways. We'll do it at night, just you and me."

The two lovers rolled onto the river beach.

"Let's practice, Harriet, for that night soon-to-come."

A smile came upon her face. He continued, "Will you become mine, now? Will you love me and share with me the joys and sorrows of life?"

"I will," she confirmed.

"Then aloha binds us to our dying days, and beyond."

Both breathed into each other. And the stream joined the glistening stars in celebration.

The couple walked down the aisle; he with a forced smile, she looking sullen. Her temperament was cold in contrast to the bright, hot, June day that stifled the congregation and curious public who filled the pews of Waine'e Church.

The wedding had been "set up," in contrast to the abomination of the other wedding that had been performed secretly at night during July of the previous year. Gossip had quickly moved through the streets of Lahaina that Kaui and Harriet had fallen into pagan ways with their union.

This had been followed by an announcement by Reverend Richards that Harriet was excommunicated. Hoapili and Kuakini, the guardians of the couple, were not happy about it either, for they, too, had been pushed into Christianity. And their kupuna had never gone as far as Richardson and his newly-arrived colleague, Richard Armstrong, in scaring Harriet about the fires of hell.

The shame of the letter of excommunication and the rumors of drinking and tobacco smoking had brought guilt to the imposed "white" part of her soul. She finally caved in.

Now she walked down the aisle of Waineʻe Church as a token to fear. It was not Kaui who walked with her away from the altar. The choice of the missionaries and Hawaiian elders was Leleiōhoku, who was quite sensitive of his role in this play. He would care for her despite the fact that he knew who her real love was, and he would slowly fade into the background, waiting in the wings as the days went by.

"Was Kaui here?" Harriet wondered. She looked up to observe the throng outside the large, arched windows. There he was, disguised as a laborer among the locals.

It was a typical Western wedding. Harriet and Leleiōhoku were off on their honeymoon to a secluded cottage in Nāpili. After a silly flurry of thrown rice, Leleiōhoku cracked at the reigns and the buggy headed north, Harriet's wedding veil flapping in the wind. Kaui untied his horse from under the shade of some large ʻulu trees and followed the carriage from a distance.

After the couple reached their destination and Harriet had discarded her gown, she told Leleiōhoku that she wished to take a walk, alone, along Nāpili Bay. The substitute groom already knew that Kaui would be waiting for her. He had seen the rider on horseback trailing them several times and offered her an excuse.

"I need to move the food supplies and clothing from the carriage and you need a break from the tensions of a wedding."

Harriet was grateful and loved Leleiōhoku, differently. Her adopted religion, however, told her that there could only be one, an ethic different from the multiple loves of her Hawaiian ancestors.

Kaui stood amidst a grove of loaded mango trees as Harriet made her way down the path to the ocean. When she saw him, she raced in his direction, flinging her arms around his neck, tears flooding her eyes.

"Why are you crying, Harriet?"

"I'm sorry, Kaui."

"About what?"

"This wedding."

"Harriet, I understand. You're not the only one who has been intimidated by these so-called men of God. You're fortunate they chose Leleiōhoku."

"I'll be able to carry on this way for awhile, Kaui, but I don't know for how long."

"Don't worry, ku'u ipo, we'll see each other a lot. I'll send for you to stay in Honolulu, and I'll come visit you at Lahaina. On official business, of course." A smile finally emerged from the new bride's face.

"Come."

"Where?"

"There's a grove of ironwoods up the hill with a carpet of needles more fragrant and satisfying than the one that runs down the aisle of Waine'e Church. After all, this is your honeymoon."

She squeezed his hand tightly as he led her along the shore and its pounding surf.

Unfortunately, Harriet was led by her predictions of failure. Not long after, to cover a propped-up marriage, Mr. Armstrong, her newly assigned spiritual counselor, suggested she drink from the waters of 'Īao. To get her away from "influences," he persuaded her to leave Lahaina for Wailuku.

The sleepy little town below Mauna Kahalewai didn't have the reputation of loose Lahaina. Her isolation increased her anxiety. It was a form of imprisonment. It was in Wailuku that she learned what would eventually cause her demise. She sent for Kaui, and he promptly sailed to Maui.

It was late afternoon. Harriet sat on a rocker tilting back and forth on the second-floor balcony of the missionary house that faced the purple peak of Pu'u Kukui. Suddenly, she heard a horse and carriage on the Kahului side of the compound. She raced down the stairs into Kaui's arms. "Oh, Kaui, how I've missed you!" She nuzzled him at the back of the head, inhaling the subtle scent of a *roselani* lei that was draped about his neck.

"I rushed as quickly as I could. Your letter had an air of urgency. Tell me."

"This is not the place. Let's take a ride out to Waihe'e. I know a beautiful spot just outside the village on the road to Kahakuloa. Just a moment. I'll grab a shawl; it will be evening in a few hours."

Minutes later they were trotting along past Waiehu, the buggy dwarfed by the tall cane stalks bordering the dusty road. They passed through the village. A few locals waved at the fancy carriage, not recognizing the male driver and female passenger. Outside the village, the road began to rise.

"Around the next corner, Kaui. There, pull the buggy over."

Kaui got out and tied the horse to an old kiawe fence post. He was awestruck by the view. Below, black rugged rocks were being attacked by the onslaught of huge, deep blue waves. He viewed arches that had been carved by the incessant pounding of the surf.

To the right, a vast meadow extended out to a rocky beach, rimmed by a line of ironwood. The cattle that had been grazing there were being called in for the night by the clanging of an old wagon wheel. Familiar with the summons to dinner, the cows followed the oldest female in the group. Her bell kept them all in single file along the carved path.

"This is a where I retreat for sanity, Kaui."

"I feel it, too, Harriet. The peacefulness is intoxicating, the kind of peace we had before 'progress.'" He paused, then asked, "Kuʻu ipo, is there a problem?"

"Actually, it's good news, I think."

"Well, enough suspense. Please tell," he said comically.

"I am with child, Kaui."

Kaui howled out a "yahoo" that echoed up the mountain and down to the shore. He grabbed under her arms and twirled her around. But he noticed that she wasn't as joyous as he was.

"What's the matter, Harriet? You seem anxious."

"I wish I could celebrate as much as you."

"We have a descendant. The lineage will continue on! *I mua, Kamehameha!* You certainly have to be excited about that?"

"Of course, I am happy about that and only wish that mother were around to share in our happiness. But … "

"But what … ?

"What will happen when the baby is born? The rumor mongers will blab that he doesn't look like Leleiōhoku."

"Why worry about what might or might not happen, Harriet?"

After a pause, she said, "Kaui, do you think I'll be a good mother?"

"That's a question every new mother asks. I'm here, by your side. I will always be here for you. You don't need to suffer alone. I want you to come back with me to Honolulu. We'll tell Leleiōhoku that you will need the best medical attention."

He kissed her, just as he had the very first time. All the nonsense that had whirled through her head seemed to disappear as she pressed against his firm body. "Let's celebrate," she said. "I just happen to have a bottle of fine Madeira in a basket in the back of the buggy. No glasses, though."

"That never stopped us before." Kaui pulled the cork, toasted the vast sea. "To our son! May he have a long and healthy life … "

" … without the hardships that have plagued ours."

"May he be happy and lead our people wisely."

Kaui handed her the bottle. "You first, my queen."

She had learned not to argue. The Madeira slipped down her throat like the quenching waters of *Kepaniwai*. She handed the bottle to him.

The *noe noe* clouds started to slip down the mountainside, as the parents-to-be finished the wine. "*Hele e Lio*," commanded Kaui. Harriet leaned tenderly on Kaui's right shoulder as the buggy began to move down the winding road back toward Wailuku.

———•••———

The ship bearing Harriet's body sailed solemnly into Lahaina Harbor. The inhabitants of Kamehameha's former capital lined the pier and stood three-deep all the way up the new road that had been built at Kaui's request.

Harriet had loved the processions of the old days, of the old ways. In her youth, she had taken every occasion to participate in parades, sometimes dressed to the gaudy hilt. Her coffin now was draped with the royal purple velvet that she and Kaui loved.

The road meandered through the groves of *hau* and breadfruit that they treasured. It wound up the side of Lahainaluna, mauka, then back down to the ocean to her final resting spot at Waineʻe. It had all happened within four months of the death of their child. The future king had only survived for a few hours after coming into this world. Was this a result of their defiance of God? Harriet had been obsessed by it in her final days.

Shortly after the death of her child, to add to her guilt, Harriet developed a high fever. Against the advice of elders, she took a cold bath, thinking it would lower her temperature. Instead, it sent the fever higher, and it never dropped. All her family and counselors

were at her side for the remaining months. She finally succumbed with Kaui at her side on what she exclaimed was one of the most beautiful mornings in Hawai'i.

The wagon bearing the coffin made its way along the last stretch into the Waine'e Street Cemetery. The body would be on the second floor of a large stone house with the mausoleum on the top. She would lie next to her child and her mother, the other Harriet, *Keōpūolani*. Unlike other mausoleums, this one was filled with light from windows facing both the majestic Mauna Kahalewai and the calm Pacific waters. Artifacts and clothing bearing the mana of royalty were on display. It was as though *Nāhi'ena'ena* were merely sleeping. But *Kauikeaouli* was relieved that his sister would no longer be in anguish, torn apart by newcomers that scorned the ancient ways,

ways that expected a brother and sister to join their flesh to keep their sacred race and lineage intact. Now she was at peace without the admonitions of missionaries and foreigners.

Kaui knew in his heart that his lover was still alive. He recalled the evening when they lay under the full moon in a rock bed made for them, scented by the nearby white ginger and lulled by the ʻĪao Stream that meandered just below their feet. The soothing memory seemed to cool the cruel sun, now at its zenith in old Lahaina.

Aloha, Sweetheart

Aloha 'oe, e Ku'u Ipo

A TONY TEXEIRA MYSTERY

The drumbeats from the Hongwanji vibrated through sleepy, sweaty Wailuku, in preparation for Saturday's *Obon* Dance of the Dead. The town's normal trades were being held hostage by the *kona* winds. When these blew, or worse, just stood still, pressure cookers of emotion were bound to explode.

In kona weather, thieves got itchy fingers, punks beefed, and dames plotted. That's probably why I was still perched in my office past closing, my underwear sticking to me like mango sap. I reached into the icebox for a Royal and pretended it was cold. The fan had *make-die-dead* a month ago. With no clients for just as long, well, I was about to go back to counting my fingers again, then call it quits and head up to the Wailuku Gardens for some round steak and onions, when…

"Tonee! Tonee Texeira!" Simplicio bellowed from the window across Market Street. "Hey, gunshoe, maybe you have business tonight?"

"It's gumshoe … gum … Simplicio, the kind you chew," I hollered back.

"Like Wiggleys?"

"Yeah, like Wiggleys."

Generally, I tried to ignore Simplicio. First of all, he lived across from my office at eyeview in a second-story cockroach trap that he shared with three other misfits. These trade-beaten planks held together by termites had always been synonymous with the

43

underbelly of Maui. It was the proverbial den of iniquity. I didn't even know Simplicio's last name. He'd come to Hawaii, incognito, among the other more honest workers to toil the sugar fields. Simplicio was, simply, a low life. Whatever criminal mischief he was involved in, I didn't care. It didn't put no bread and jelly on my table.

"Hey, Tony P.I., maybe tonight is your lucky night!"

"What do you mean?"

"You got one client."

I looked at the Peters Mortuary 1939 calendar. Every square up to and including July 13 stood naked.

"Whatchyoumean?"

"Look, somebody coming!"

I leaned out the window. There, wafting toward the office, shrouded in the glow of twilight, was Leilani Lau, her luxurious hula curves barely contained by her red satin Chinese dress, an inviting slit running the length of her luscious gam. She pressed her long probing finger into the street buzzer. It gargled. I jumped to the door, pushed up my tie from bellybutton to neck, and blotted the perspiration that had pooled on my forehead.

"Come on up!"

The apparition ascended the stairs.

"Tony? Tony Texeira?"

"Yeah, who's calling?"

"An old friend."

"Can't be. I don't have any friends."

I was pulling Leilani's leg, of course. I knew the dame. In fact, I knew her when she was good. And when she was good, she was very, very good. But, foolishly, Leilani wanted to be a rich man's pup, and so she was living the life with Red Lau and all his wrong numbers.

"Tony," she said, as she leaned into me. The sultry body was previewed by a whiff of white ginger, giving me something close to a non-kiss. "Long time no see."

"Yeah."

My emotions gushed like a flash flood in ʻĪao Stream. The Star Ice mercury on the wall seemed to go up a few degrees. Beads of love dew flowed down and disappeared into her cleavage. Luckily, pessimism saved me. I weakly resisted.

"I need your help, Tony."

"Why'd you come to me? I'm just a small dick. Go see Alexander. Red can afford him."

"It's about Red. Something's up, but I don't know what it is. Alexander is too clean and high *maka-maka* for someone like Red."

"So you came for leftovers?"

"No, I came because ... I trust you." Trust meant one thing to me in these dog-eat-dog streets—a word that starts with T.

"Would $500 do for an opener?"

At this moment in my life, even a buck sounded erotic. It meant cold beers again. I played it cool, like I had to actually think about it. I couldn't resist the five hundred bucks, or Leilani for that matter. Something was afoot, though. Something was rotten in Wailuku.

"We had a little argument about where he'd been at all hours of the night. The rumor is he's been hanging out with Simplicio."

I checked across the street. Binoculars peered through the closed flimsy gossamer curtain that was usually opened after it blocked out the morning rays from Haleakalā. Simplicio seemed interested in this *wahine*.

She continued.

"After he left, I found his little black book and under today's date was scrawled, 'Maui Grand Hotel, Room 213.' That's all I know."

I doubted that. I was no pushover but played along.

"You gotta help me, Tony. It looks like trouble."

"Trouble is my business."

"Does that mean yes?"

"Make the check out to Tony Texeira."

She reached into her red silk dragon purse, pulled out a checkbook, and scribbled my name and the total of the last five months rent on a

piece of paper that might possibly be worthless. We'd see. I knew she lived beyond her means in Sprecklesville, among the wealthy. She ripped the check, handed it to me, stood up, and sauntered to the door.

"Be careful, Tony. You know I always had something for you."

She glided down the stairs and disappeared into the twilight.

The sun was setting behind the West Maui Mountains. My first destination—the Maui Grand Hotel—was Maui's finest, a two-story white Victorian with first and second floor porches that wrapped around three-quarters of the building. Large green palms shaded the rocking chairs, with Ming vases and copper spittoons for visitors.

A circular drive off of Main Street fronted its grand entry stairs. Local people didn't stay here. It was for haoles with money. So if Red Lau was here, even temporarily, he'd have to be in the bucks. I walked onto the green Moroccan rug in the lobby.

"Vagrants not allowed," sneered Kats Katsuka from behind the desk.

"Don't get your panties twisted, Kats. It's business."

"Red Lau. 213."

I didn't have to surmise how he knew. Behind that starched shirt, tailored coat, and tie was Mr. Nīele, himself. He should've been a *Maui News* reporter; he knew everyone's movements in town. Kats added, "Oh, and Tony, I wish you'd meet with your type someplace off the property. Bad for the clientele, you know."

I bit my lip. What a punk! It's hard to believe this dummy slug was from a sweet old Maui family. I headed up the winding staircase to the second floor. As I creaked along the teakwood floors, I speculated on the meaning of the 13 in Room 213.

I banged my fist on the door and waited. No response. I rapped again, even louder. Still no answer. I jiggled the knob. I could open it a little, but there was a weight against the door. I called in, "Red? Red?" He didn't answer. I pushed again and managed to force my head through the opening, then my whole body. Now I knew why Red never answered. He was now officially a doorstop, a dead one. I had to take a peek at the body before I got outa there. It was a bullet at close range to the chest, the kinda hole a 38'd leave. When I turned to skidaddle, I ran right into a beer barrel of gray.

It was to be my "dear" friend, the rarely honest Sergeant Patsy O'Sullivan. O'Sullivan's pact with the rich foreigners was that once he'd been helped into position, he would scratch their ʻōkoles. But after the sugar barons moved back to Frisco, Patsy turned to small compensations for street transactions.

"Stick em up," he barked like a rouge-faced bulldog, as he got himself into Room 213. There he saw Red on the green carpet, a pool of blood oozing from his technicolor aloha shirt.

"Lay off, Patsy. I didn't do it. I just … "

"Yeah, you just happen to be standing over a dead body … "

"He was here when I got … Talk to Kats … "

"He called me. He said you were up to something with Red."

"Why that … Come on. It's a .38 puka. You know I carry a .45. And besides, I wouldn't have had time. I just got here. Ask Kats … "

"How long does it take to fire a gun, huh, gumshoe?"

"As fast as Kats could before I arrived."

"Well, why would a successful desk clerk at a fancy hotel do something like that?"

"For the money, just like you."

He poked me with his stick.

"Quit yappin'. You should talk. Go on, Tony, tell me why you had to leave the H.P.D. Something about corrupt cops, eh Texeira? You tell me all about it up at the jailhouse. Oh, and hand over your gat. I went down sniffing sticky finger coppers like you."

He cracked me across the face with his nightstick.

"Gee. It looks like Red and you had a fight. Did he slug you on the right side of your face too?" The human donut made a second mark with his billy club. I crouched down on the floor in pain.

"Seems you retaliated against Mr. Lau for those nasty blows you gave him for not paying up on that opium deal."

"What opium deal?" I mumbled.

Realizing a stupid slip, he roared, "Shut the hell up!" He shoved me out into the hallway. Kats scampered away from the keyhole, his usual place of residence. He curled his lip at me as I was pushed out the lobby, down the stairs, and up the street to the station, a block away, up Wells. Bernie was on duty at the front desk.

Patsy croaked. "Book 'em Bernie! He can pay his $400 bail in the morning." I cringed. I fantasized the money flying out of my pocket. I'd have $100 left.

"Tony! What you in for this time?"

"Murder! And, Bernie, don't let him out till I say."

Patsy did a 180 and headed out into Wailuku's kinda mean streets.

"He's gotta be kidding?"

"Red Lau went down, and I'm taking the rap."

Bernie knew the game. We had grown up together in Mill Camp, and he and I knew who the rotten mangoes were. Even "Bernie the Bruiser" had been on the take for a while but, with a failing kidney from bad pineapple hooch over the years, he'd turned soft.

"Should I call the kid, Tony?"

"Call the kid, Bernie. Call the kid."

The kid was Tedo De La Cruz.

"Kinda sad that you have to call a kid attorney to help you out."

"He's the best, Bernie. That kid's gonna be a great three-piece suit someday."

"You trust him?" There was that trust word again.

"Call him. He's at Zita's."

I headed over to empty jail cell number one. There was only one cell. As I waited for Tedo, I loosened my tie, kicked off my shoes, and dozed in the hot cell. A little brown fan in the corner teased me with its manini hint of air.

"Tonee! Tonee!"

Tedo was here.

He chuckled, "What's the matter, Tony? You kill somebody?"

"Yeah!…I mean…no! I was framed!"

"No shit, Tonee! Who went down?"

Bernie yelled, "Hey, nona that crap in here, Tedo. Just because…"

I cut Bernie off. "Look I got $30 here for you to go check on some things."

"How many errands for thirty bucks?"

"Oh, about five or six."

"Tony, you gotta be pullin' my leg. That's at least three hours. A guy's gotta live nowadays. Be sensible. Remember, I'm cheaper than Alexander."

"Tedo, do you know what a depression is? Oh, hey, Tedo, you got one smoke?"

"What do you think I am, Tony? I'm a kid!"

He pulled out a pack of Chesterfields and thrust it in my face. A match followed.

"Okay, Tony. I'll make you a deal. Twenty smacks now and twenty after I've nailed *da baggah*."

"Okay, okay."

I detached the remaining twenty from my now empty wallet.

"Here's what you gotta dig for."

Tedo pulled out a stubby little pencil and a weathered, multi-creased grocery list with the Main Market letterhead.

"First, check out the whereabouts for the last twenty-four hours of the following characters: Kats Katsuka, Sergeant O' Sullivan, Red Lau, Simplicio … whatever his name is, and Leilani Lau."

"Oh, oh … a woman! Go ahead … "

"Find out who owned the .38. Check the Laus' financial situation …"

Tedo gleefully sliced into my list with, "… and their insurance policies."

"Yeah and don't forget to check the departure lists of the Pan Am *Baby Clipper*, the Lurline … You know, anything outbound … Got it?"

"Okey, dokey, boss man." He stood there frozen, his arm bent and his palm open.

"Okay, okay. Don't push." I slapped Jackson's green face into Tedo's clammy palm. Sherlock, or was it Shylock, gleefully barreled out the door into the sweaty twilight.

The big clock clanged quits. Bernie gathered his stuff. He usually left straight home on the sixth gong of the big Bulova above his head. Poor Bernie was counting the minutes he had to live.

"Say, Bernie, before you leave, could you turn on the Philco? By the way, where's Meyer for his shift?"

"Probably at Hanaoka's Lunch Counter. I'll honk at him when I go by … and don't try anything funny while there's no one here … promise?!"

"Relax, Bernie. Go on home."

"I'll check you out in the morning." Bernie waddled out the door.

I faded into dreamland from the *Your Hit Parade* countdown on the Philco. A big fat moon sat atop the mango trees framed by a small porthole-like window looking out the back courtyard of the jail.

—— · ——

I wasn't there with Tedo, but since I'd been through this routine a thousand times before, I might as well have been sitting on his shoulder.

Tedo would head down Market from Main to Happy Valley. From those streets and the uncles, aunties, and cousins who walked it, Tedo was confident that all his questions would be answered. Tony, too, knew in his gut, that it was Leilani, considering her past entanglement in seedy, turncoat affairs. It would be another thing to prove it on paper. The white bosses in power always wanted "the *pepa*."

Tedo would first hit Aunty Hattie Pumba. He skidded his bike in front of the large window blazoned "First Insurance of Maui." As he entered, he caught his lovable but dizzy Aunty Hattie finishing her own personal conversation.

"I have to leave a message for the boss … the Ah Sing account … now where's that pencil? Bon dance tonight …" Hattie looked up finally recognizing her nephew. "Ay, Tedo. I didn't know that was you. Why aren't you in school?"

"Aunty, it's way past two o'clock. In fact, it's pau work."

"Oh, that's right, Tedo. I've been a little busy … Where is that pencil?"

"It's behind your ear."

She laughed apologetically. "Oh, yeah. How observant, jell like Sherlock Jones. I know you'll make a great detective some day. So, Tedo, what can I do for you?"

Tedo, in anticipation of a no, nevertheless, said, "I need some … info … "

"Are you doing stuff for Tony again?" She gathered up her belongings. "That guy! So sad he have to use one high school kid to be his Della Streep."

"You know I need the practice if I going be that great detective. Besides, you know Tony, he always pay."

"I told you, Tedo, how many times. We're not supposed to give out information about our clients. Besides, what will I get out of this? … Only trouble. I gotta go, Tedo. Mano must be all mad that he neva get suppa yet. I told him last night mo easy we go Bon dance and buy chow fun." Hattie grabbed her purse and headed to the door. Tedo raced to the position, blocking her from leaving.

"Speaking of chow fun. I know what will convince you to assist Maui's future defense attorney," he continued enticingly. "One dozen, yes, twelve of Zita's fat, delicious pasteles."

Her hand stopped short from shutting off the lights. "How many?" She said, lured by Tedo's mom's prize-winning delicacies.

"Twelve."

"And when delivered?"

Tedo had her in his clutch. "Tomorrow, just in time for dinner."

She headed back to the files. "Okay, okay, what's the name?"

He thrust his hand out with the list and leaned over Aunty's back as she perused the files.

"Simplicio. I don't know his last name."

"You mean that sleezeball from up the street? Nope."

Tedo continued. "Sergeant O'Reilly."

"That guy should go on a diet."

"Kats Katsuka."

"That tightwad? All his insurance money's in a shoe box under his bed." She paused for a second. "Curious … ?"

"What's up, Aunty?"

"Mano was buying boiled peanuts at Uncle Toshi's stand at the K. O. Pagan—Mike Wade fight at the fairgrounds Sataday when he saw Kats and O'Reilly having an intense *wala'au* behind the bleachers. He told me that there was some strange odd couple. How are all these guys connected? What's this all about, Tedo?"

"Verrry interesting, as Inspector Chan says. So what about Red Lau, Leilani Lau?"

"Oh, that's easy."

"What do you mean?"

"They were here about a month ago for change their policy." She dug for the file.

"How'd they change it?"

"Now you know, Tedo, I can't tell you that."

"But if you moved over a little … I might accidentally see it." As Aunty shifted, Tedo's eye focused on the entry—$50,000.

Hattie slammed the file drawer. "Okay, nuff. I gotta go before Mano get pupule."

She grabbed her belongings and headed for the door.

Tedo lovingly thanked her. "Oh, by the way, Aunty, have you seen cousin Chico lately?"

"Tedo, I no like you associating with him, even if he is blood. I know he's out of O'ahu Prison. Why what you want see him for?"

"Not social. Have to do with the case."

"You be careful, boy. I saw him headed down Happy Valley this morning."

Tedo headed out the door, stuck his head back in, and whispered, "Mahalo, Aunty."

As I lay on that sweaty cot, I presumed that the Puerto Rican Ellery Queen would check with his cousin, Chico, about the drug connection. After that he'd have to race to the travel office on Lower Main before it closed to check out if anyone was flying the coop.

A large Tootsie Roll and Baby Ruth sign suggested the name of the old shack just a few minutes by bike from Happy Valley. But the "Candy Store" was nothing of the kind. It was the local opium den. As Tedo rode up on his bike, Bully, the bodyguard, rose from the dilapidated, shredded couch that sat on the rickety porch.

He yelled out, "Sorry. No kids allowed!"

"I know that, Bully, but I gotta see Chico. There's an emergency at home."

"I'll see if he's available. Stay by that bike and no monkey business. You sabe?"

"Me sabe, kimosabe."

As Bully entered the shack, two men, obviously drugged, exited. One gave stink-eye to Tedo. "What you lookin' at, boy?"

Tedo changed the direction of his glance.

"Da smokers getting younger," said the other addict as they walked past Tedo.

Chico exited with Bully. The latter pointed the boy out and retreated back into the den.

"Tedo, what the hell you doing here?" argued Chico as he approached the bike.

"Ah sorry, Cousin Chico … but it's a matter of life and death. The cops have Tony Texeira in the calaboose on a bum rap."

"Here, come, " said Chico as he led Tedo under the shade of the towering mango trees.

"I dunno why you came to me. I had nutting to do wid dat."

"I know that … but it does have something to do with your pastime."

"Look, I pau dat violence stuff."

"But you still puff … so can you tell me about an opium deal that went down lately. I figure it's Simplicio."

"Dat monkey's behind? He would send his madda up the riva if he could. And you bettah no tell anybody this. He was Red's supplia."

"Red Lau is not going to smoke opium anymore. Somebody bumped him off and Tony's in trouble. C'mon, Chico."

"Okay, okay. I heard tru the grapevine that Simplicio picked up about 5000 smacks of the poppy. But I no trust the bum. He bad business; stay away from that bugga. Now go. And rememba, you never see me." Bully stepped out onto the porch. "Quick, now. Get the hell."

Tedo jumped on the bike like Gene Autrey hopped on Champion. "See you, Uncle."

Chico yelled back, "Later, Cuz."

Tedo hightailed it to Lower Main. He had to know who was getting out of town and then try to get back to the pawn shop to check out who had purchased the .38 to frame Tony.

Tedo was only a teen but his heart throbbed like a stubbed toe everytime he ran into Noe Shibuya. She was as good looking as his Hollywood beauties like Paulette Goddard. He nervously leaned the bike up against the travel agency wall, took a deep breath, and faced his dream.

"Tedo, what brings you here? Going traveling?"

"I ... I need some help."

"Are you working for Tony again? Our last date ended with beer all over my new dress. That guy ... Anyway, what's the case?"

"Tony's in the hoosegow."

"What ... spill the beans ... what's the case?"

"I can't right now. I'm in a rush. I need to know if any of these are intending to skip town: Kats Katsuka, Officer O'Reilly, Simplicio what's his name, or Leilani Lau."

"The *Baby Clipper* left earlier today with none of them on it. The only thing leaving tonight is a freighter out of Kahului. Here's the list; look for yourself." His eyes glowed when he spotted the name.

Tedo ran to the door, stopped, turned and in a romantic tone, whispered, "Thank you, Noe." This was followed by a blaring, "I gotta go check a gun out."

Noe stood puzzled as her teen admirer pumped hard up Main Street, hoping to get to Shakes' pawn shop before it closed.

Luck wasn't with Tedo on that one. The now-darkened sky confirmed that all the Wailuku businesses were closed. Everyone was at the Bon dance. My junior detective would let me have a night of shut-eye and stop by to talk to Shakes in the morning. Besides, I'm sure Tedo would be hungry. Even I salivated at the thought of a heap of Zita's corned beef and gravy, raw onions with Hawaiian salt, and poi.

I woke up from the little movie of Tedo's snooping by the incessant chattering of some myna birds, my clothes one big dishrag from the heat. Bernie came into focus.

"Bernie, you still here?"

"I came and went, Tony. It's morning. Patsy says you're allowed to go, with bail, of course. You want some java?"

"Wanna poison me before you set me free?" I grabbed the now crumpled check that I slept with and unwillingly surrendered it. "I need a hundred back, Bernie. The check's for five."

Bernie grabbed some twenties as he threw the doomed check into the bail cashbox. I was now ahead by only 80 clams, including Tedo's first cut.

"By the way, did Tedo come by yet?" Speaking of the devil, Tedo's bike skidded in front of the police station.

"So, where's the rest of my retainer, Texeira?"

"Is that all you think about?"

I painfully extracted another twenty from the remaining eighty. Tedo turned over the written scraps of evidence. "Still got any of those Chesterfields?"

I waved off Bernie and took Tedo out to the shady palms that front the Bishop National Bank. After moments of anxious quiet, Tedo finally blurted out, "So, have we solved it?"

"I solved it, Tedo. Did you?"

"Who do you think I am? Some lousy flatfoot? Here's the scoop. Red Lau made a deal with Simplicio to purchase fifty grand of opium from some Chinese from Waihe'e. They made an appointment at the Wailuku Grand. But Lau didn't take the money with him. He would pay Simplicio after he saw the stuff. He called Leilani to bring the cash over. She also brought, according to Shake's ledger, a .38. She plugged her darling husband after she got there. Simplicio arrived, saw the corpse, and hightailed back with the opium to Waihe'e with apologies to the suppliers."

"The insurance … ?"

"They had a $50,000 insurance policy on each other. I think they call that a clear 'motive' in all the Ellery Queens I read."

"Exactly. And Kats? I presume he was involved to set me up."

"Aunty Hattie said that her husband, Mano, saw him, Kats, and O'Reilly yacking it up at the fights, and Zita said he was buzzing with Leilani in front of the showroom window of Von HammYoung, supposedly looking at the new Packards. And then, later in the day, she caught them yacking some more in front of the new *Gunga Din* posters at the 'Īao Theater."

"He surely was her eyes at the hotel for a substantial reward … and for setting me up for the fuzz."

"Looks like Patsy was paid to catch me at the scene of the crime and not let me out till morning."

"So that Leilani would be in international waters, sailing on the *Oriental Star* to Hong Kong. You know, Tony, it's just as I figured from the beginning … it was that dame."

I squashed the cigarette out. "You hungry, Tedo?"

"Hey, I'm a kid. I'm hungry all the time."

"I have a craving for round steak and onions. How's that sound to you?"

"For breakfast?"

"For breakfast."

Several months later I got a card from Leilani from an undisclosed location in Singapore, a country without extradition, confirming her guilt. The postscript read, " Tony, you know I always had something for you. *Aloha 'oe, e ku'u ipo.*"

The sun now escaped the clutch of Haleakalā and was burning up old Wailuku town, everyone yearning for those pleasant trades of late October. For today, however, the konas would remain. It was going to be another scorcher.

Aunty Becky's Tavern

Ka Hale Inu Lama o 'Anakē Becky

It was a night to have a girl with you. The moon was large. The trade winds from the northeast, which should have started cooling by now—early December—were still balmy. Pā'ia Bay was a giant, placid mirror reflecting the fluffy whites being seduced by the West Maui Mountains. A man in uniform bent over, cupped his hands, and lit up a Camel.

"Eh, the enemy going see that stupid cigarette and you going start World War II," Joe admonished the smoker.

"No be silly," Val replied. "Even if had Japanese submarines out there, they couldn't see this little glow. Looks like all we doing is making sure the barge from Honolulu no *huli* in the harbor. Eh, and forget about the Japanese. I no think their subs can hold enough gasoline to make it all the way from Tokyo."

"What? You think the brass would stick us here in this bunker for nutting."

The two young reservists came again to an awkward quiet. They stared out across the way. Soft rolling waves underlined the lights of Wailuku. Val swore he could see Uncle Willy's lantern, all the way out at Kahakuloa, leading his cows in for the night. The uneasiness in Val and Joe's silence forced them to meditate on the possibility that they had made a mistake in signing up for the reserve to make an extra fifty dollars a month. Now there was a good chance they'd be heading out to Europe if the war called them.

"What's today's date, anyway?" Joe blurted out.

Val jumped. "Hey, come in slow from the silence!"

"Oh, sorry, Val. You want me ring one bell to ease you out of your coma?"

"It's nineteen days before Christmas."

"Twenty-five minus nineteen." Joe scrawled "Dec. 6, '41" on the bunker wall.

"Ho, lucky we get tomorrow off. What you going do, Joe?"

"I gotta help my mom-folks set up the Christmas crèche at St. Joseph Church."

"I'll swing by and say hello to your folks. We'll be out that way. I'm taking Makaleka up to Kula for a ride. My father, that Scrooge, wen' finally buck-a-loose the car keys for tomorrow. He only agreed after I had filled his jam glass with the vino three times."

"What, when you going marry that wahine?"

"In June, hopefully."

The slapping of the combers against the bunker seemed to ease Val into thoughts of his coming marriage. Makaleka was everything he wanted. She was beautiful; he knew she would be a great mother. He imagined his boys, now teens, playing baseball, his sport. She'd just graduated from Lahainaluna, and her family had moved from Wahikuli, above Lahaina, to Wailuku. Her parents had scrimped and saved to move the family to "the city."

"No forget now … "

Val came to attention. "Forget what?"

"The place where we meet every Saturday night, if we don't pull reserves, again."

"Grab your stuff. The next judges for the invisible submarine races going be here soon."

They could see the two figures of the next watch moving down the beach. As they made their way up the trail, Joe stopped. "After you get married, Makaleka going still let you hang out with the boys at Aunty Becky's?"

"She betta."

The two soldiers of the 298th Division exchanged small talk with the fresh sentries and disappeared into the darkness of the ironwood grove.

"Val, *pehea ʻoe?*" Aunty Becky called out.

"*Maikaʻi*, Aunty, *maikaʻi*," greeted Val as he wrapped his arms around his and every soldier's substitute mom.

"Where's Joe?"

"Not here yet. So good to see you guys no foget each adda."

"I'm concerned about Joe…"

"I know…you don't have to tell me. That car accident made him bitter."

"I think I would feel the same if I lost one arm. He no like the thought that he gotta sit home while we go off to war."

"Mo bettah stay. No get guarantee any soldier going come home. Joe only lost his arm; the rest of his body still useful … Speaking of the devil!"

Joe called from across the room, pointing to Aunty Becky's Kīhei establishment, "Take a good look, Val. You won't see it for at least two years."

Val looked around the old Quonset hut. He'd miss the mourning doves that lodged themselves over the arch beams, the gravel floor with long *lūʻau* tables, the jukebox that played *Don't Sit Under the Apple Tree* when you kicked it hard enough, some of the best *pūpū* and poi in the territory, and Aunty's collection of beers from around the world. He'd miss, of course, Aunty Becky the most. She, like Duke Kahanamoku, was Maui's official ambassador to the U.S. Military.

Despite all the drinking and swinging elbows that took place at Aunty Becky's Tavern, it was never the site of a John Wayne-type military brawl between the branches. She wouldn't allow it, and beware any soldier who crossed the line! Aunty Becky's stink eye was something to be reckoned with. That's not to say that there weren't any fisticuffs or black eyes among the men in uniform. They'd duke it out across the street in the county park that would be named after Mayor Sam. There in the shadows of the thorny kiawe, beyond the ballfield, away from the eyes of Tūtū Becky, they'd beef.

"I'll get you boys some beer, special kind brought back from some of my boys in Germany. They captured one nest that sat on top one old brewery and, naturally, spent the night suckin' 'em up. These come highly recommended."

She left the two friends to catch up. Joe continued his conversation. "You so lucky, Val. You still heading out Tuesday?"

"Yeah, we'll be at Schofield for about six weeks. We should be leaving for Guadalcanal in November."

November would be just short of one year since Val and the still-intact Joe sat together in that quiet bunker on Pā'ia Bay.

"Guadalcanal? Where the hell is that? Why do we always fight in places not even on a map?"

Val got as academic as a Quiz Kid. "Guadalcanal, one of the islands of the Solomon Group—native name: Isatabu; location: Pacific Ocean, nine degrees, thirty-seven minutes south, 160 degrees, eleven minutes east; largest city: Honiara. Want any more?"

Facetiously, Joe added, "Highest Point?"

Imitating Franklin Delano Roosevelt, "Mt. Popomanaseu, of course!"

"I'm impressed!"

"Well, I asked myself the same question: Where the hell is this place? So I whipped out the *Encyclopedia Brittanica* and found out for myself."

"I guess you've been following the *Star-Bulletin*. The Marines have done the dirty work. That should make it a little safer for you."

Aunty Becky made her way to the table, balancing a mound of *pāpaʻi*, fish cake, boiled peanuts, and a couple of the German lagers.

"*ʻAi a hewa a ka waha, o ka leo ka uku,*" Aunty chanted.

"You know that one?"

"Eat until your mouth can have no more. Right, Aunty?" Val interpreted.

"*Maikaʻi.* Good. Keep talking *ʻŌlelo Hawaiʻi.* We must preserve it."

Aunty plopped the food down on the light green table.

"This more better than those A-B-C, whatever alphabet, rations. Might as well eat cardboard. Myron went down Keawakapu with the galvanized tubs. He said he stayed up all night listening to this bambutcha crabs fall into the tins, scratching hopelessly to get out."

She looked at Joe and said in a whisper, "Oh, and two bowls rice. I made special since you my regular customers and your good buddy here not going see this for … "

With a sad face, she stopped. "How long we not going see you, Val?"

He tried to downplay the drama.

"Eh, Aunty, before you know it, I going be back. Just make sure you get enough food for my welcome-home party."

"Last chance for see the sunset before blackout!" someone yelled from the front. The servicemen at the bar grabbed their beers and headed out to the benches that faced Kihei Bay. Val got nostalgic as they exited the front door.

"Best sunset in the world," he claimed, sucking at a crab and sipping his Bavarian beer.

"Your wife-to-be would argue with your sunset claim. And she might be right—that her hometown boasts the best. That's one reason why the Aliʻi made Lahaina their home."

The profiles of soldiers and civilians turned orange as the sun dropped down like a coin in a slot behind the McGregor Point Lighthouse on the *pali* cliffs. As dusk settled, Aunty Becky hugged her two boys around their backs.

"Okay, boys, back into the tavern before the M.P.s come check. And I need some help, as usual, dropping the black drapes over all the puka!"

Although they temporarily felt like prisoners in their own house, after several beers, all would be forgotten by the camaraderie.

"Too much beer and crab," complained Joe, patting his ʻōpū. He slowly rose and headed toward the lua. Aunty Becky was back in the kitchen banging dirty dishes in the wash sink. Val straddled one of the benches, reminiscing with an old Maui High classmate, occasionally staring up at the huge, tin Lucky Strike sign that showed a couple enjoying a cigarette. He decided to do the same. He wove his way through the double black curtains out the front door and looked across to the park.

"What the hell?!" he said, his mouth opened wide. Everything was ink black. On Maui, even, a moonless night was usually brightened by the stars over Kihei. But tonight it was as though a large black curtain had covered the whole island.

He wandered across the road and walked out into the park toward the ocean. There was no one and, even stranger, no M.P.s. Where were they? The local military was still jittery, even a year after Pearl Harbor.

The rules were so tough that some local Japanese were under scrutiny, despite the fact that they had gathered immediately after the attack on Pearl Harbor at Baldwin High School's Auditorium and declared their loyalty. The gruff, non-local military police, to protect their racism, would mumble in mocking pidgin, "You lucky you not California. There you go internment camp."

Suddenly a sergeant ran out from the inky blackness. "Have you got the atabrine?" he yelled.

"Atabrine? What's that?" Val was confused.

"How long have you been here? Did you just get off the boat?"

"I haven't been on a …" Val was cut off halfway through.

"Where's your uniform, private? What the hell are you doing running around Henderson Field in an aloha shirt in the middle of all this chaos?"

"Henderson Field?" Val thought. "Henderson?" That didn't make sense.

Henderson was the name of the airstrip at Guadalcanal. That's where the 298th Infantry would be stationed. He'd be Sergeant of the Service Company. The grizzly sergeant was talking about the future and it was happening now.

"Atabrine!" the sergeant yelled at him.

Finally, out of the avalanche of training terms, he remembered Atabrine. "We don't handle medications out of Service Company."

"That was Schofield, soldier. Where the hell do you think you are, in class? This is the real world. We do what we can. He's out there in the jungle, heaving, hot as the day, in the dark. The poor man is dying from malaria. Go find some atabrine!"

Val was confused. Where would he would run to? He knew he had to get out of this nightmare. "I'll be back as soon as possible."

He headed to what he thought was Kihei Bay, but because of the complete blackness he wasn't sure which was which. Then he came across a young marine, standing, staring into the pitch. "Hey, buddy!" Val called out to whom he thought was a drunken sailor who had wandered out of Aunty Becky's into the park as he had. A tortured face filled with disillusion, and anger, turned.

"Another cream puff! Johnny come lately!" the man cursed.

"Cream puffs? What do you mean?"

"Why not come next year or, better yet, after the signing of the armistice."

Below them, in the shadows was the body of a twisted soldier, with a half face.

"He was my best buddy. We fought alongside each other when we took Lunga Point. I guess you heard—that our supplies were cut off. Only fourteen days of food. Bombarded eighty-nine times at last count. Those fourteen-inch shells were definitely going to hit one of us. Lucky him. He doesn't have to see hell on earth anymore. If it wasn't for the mosquitoes and the filth, he could have made it home. He took on that severe strain of dysentery and his once-fit body was never the same. The slightest mistake in diet would eventually bring on personal humiliation. He was embarrassed—a marine shitting in his pants."

Val finally figured out what a "cream puff" was—those who had come as a mop-up team after some very bloody battles. He wanted to tell the depressed marine that he wasn't the commandant; he didn't decide when he could come or go, fight or not fight. He was just a grunt from Maui. He suddenly remembered his future. Val wanted to tell the hero that stood before him that it wasn't no cake walk getting into Henderson Field, that the transport he was flying in with dozens of saucer-eyed kids had taken severe flak as they approached the airstrip, named after one of the first casualties of Midway. He could hear "Our Fathers" and "Hail Marys" being mumbled as the Japanese pounded their aircraft.

"There's a beautiful grove of mango trees over there," said the marine, as he pointed into the velvet black. "I think Mac would want to sleep in peace there."

He grabbed his friend by the arms and dragged him off to his final resting place. Normally, the fence of large cement blocks and barbed wire that protected the beach from a possible invasion could be seen at night. This play on a darkened stage confirmed to Val he surely wasn't on Maui, much less Kansas, anymore. He had stepped into his future warlike Oz.

A tall, emaciated, Brillo-headed, brown man and two small boys, his sons most likely, stepped forward out of the dark. They stopped and stared at each other, speechless.

"You American?" he uttered.

"I'm American," Val confirmed. "Val Rodrigues."

He extended his hand.

"Daniel Pule…my sons, Jacob and Samuel." Val felt his rough hand.

"You come from Texas?"

"No, Hawai'i."

The three natives looked at each other and smiled. The adult stepped forward and grabbed Val, hugging him. Val recoiled at the stranger. "My brother live Hilo. Where from, you?"

"I am a Maui boy."

"Beautiful, says brother. Your mountain almost as big as Mauna Kea. Hali … Hale … "

" … Haleakalā."

Val confirmed and smiled back at the odds of running into someone who knew what a Hilo was.

"Rain plenty there."

Val now knew this guy was the real McCoy.

"How did your brother live Hilo?"

"Before war, insects destroy many trees. Brother fed up. Not too good fisherman to stay. Took boat to Hawai'i. Work for sugar cane plantation. I should have gone too. Lived Cape Esperance. Shells fell and killed my wife and little girls. As soldiers say, caught in middle."

"Where do you live now?" said Val, sadly predicting the answer.

"All over island. We keep move away from bombs. Things getting better, though. Less fighting. We wait for everybody to go before back to normal."

Val was moved by the mettle of a man who had lost his wife and girls and home. How would Val have reacted? What would have been his state of mind? What if he had lost Makaleka and the children that he looked forward to? He wanted to give him something. He reached inside his pockets. There were only a couple of coins, and he handed them over to the boys. He stuck out a pack of Camel cigarettes. "This is all I have."

"You have at least three? One for me and my sons?"

"This not for children," Val cautioned.

"These not children anymore. Children's age in years, yes. But this war makes them adult way before. Malaria, land mines—them more serious concern than moment of pleasure. Be safe. And say hello to my brother in Hilo."

The tall man and boys walked in a new direction as Val called out, "What's your brother's name?" They disappeared before answering.

String of Pearls? Glenn Miller? Where was that coming from? He followed the music.

Now, slightly visible again, was Aunty Becky's Tavern. He was home. He laughed awkwardly at the thought that he had wandered off to Guadalcanal. He opened the tavern door and slipped through the double black curtains.

"Where were you?" called out Aunty from the back.

"Out having a smoke."

"Boy, you going be taken away by the M.P.s."

"I was safe. I did it in the tool shed."

"Good boy. Ass my favorite place too."

"Where's Joe?"

Aunty Becky looked at him puzzled.

"Stop pulling my leg, Val. You know what happened when you were fighting in Guadalcanal."

What was she talking about? Val quickly gazed at the Maui Dry Goods calendar on the wall. It was December 1943. A year had disappeared. He repeated again. "Where's Joe?"

"Come on, Val. You know his depression took the better of him. The loss of his arm, not being able to go with buddies like you into battle. He told me once, 'The biggest story the world has ever seen was taking place, and I was sitting on the sideline.'"

"Aunty, I'm confused. When I went out the door, it was 1942, and when I returned, it was a year later."

Val expected any normal person to doubt his sanity. But this was Aunty Becky.

"Did you see the war?"

He hesitatingly said, "I did."

"And did you see its horrors?"

"How did…?"

"You think I'm one prophet? Hardly! Lost both husband in World War I and now Malcolm in World War II. War is sadness and cruelty and death. But now no more, Val. No more malaria, no more jungles, no more bodies mutilated by mortar, no more casualties at home."

I'm sitting on one of the few remaining concrete standards that held the razor wire that lined Kalama Park during the war years. The sun is gilding everything copper-orange like the day Joe, Aunty Becky, and the boys and I shared that final time in silence watching the sun sink slowly into the sea.

There's a big game on TV—the tourists have gone for the summer, the beach, quiet. Those sons I dreamed about who would play baseball someday, did, and went to the National Championship in Anaheim. They gave me a couple of grandchildren and have settled into their challenges and rewards with good paying jobs in Silicon Valley.

Aunty Becky's gone; the tavern of yesterday replaced by a tourist trap. Makaleka left us earlier than expected. And soon I'll be gone. But I rest assured that even after my passing, those bountiful clouds will roll, like the rushing waves below, toward the longer lasting white sand and green peaks of my Valley Isle.

An Island
Beyond Hōkūleʻa

He Moku i ʻōnei o Hōkūleʻa

Jeannie Booth tootled down Haleakalā to make her *Maui News* deadline. The stars were the only streetlights on the black mountain. She was doubting whether she would make it to Wailuku on time. Her stomach was growling; the pūpū at the ranger station rededication had been pretty meager.

She didn't need more caffeine, but, desperate, Jeannie pulled out her thermos and guzzled some of the lukewarm coffee. She'd been the last person to leave the park entrance. The U.S. Secretary of the Interior was visiting Maui—it was a rare event for a federal mucky muck to make a trip to the Territory. Jeannie had cornered him about how things might change after Hawaiʻi became the forty-ninth state. His TPA flight, however, was leaving shortly and, since it was the last one, he only had an hour to get down the 10,000-foot volcano to the airport.

The two on-duty rangers escorted the VIP to Kahului, and gave Jeannie the assignment to turn out the ranger station lights. As she stepped out into the dark night, she acutely sensed that she was the only human now atop one of the world's largest volcanos. She had a hard time starting her Fairlane station wagon, named Nelliebelle after Roy Rogers' sputtering jeep.

She figured it was because of the high altitude. Others had insisted that Nelliebelle was, simply, a pile of rolling junk, and that she should trade the clunker in for a horse. But Jeannie loved her Ford. It made her feel like Bogie, a female Sam Spade. As a plus, on an island of just 50,000 people, everybody knew her by her moving Spam can. They'd point and say, "There go Jeannie and Nelliebelle!"

Suddenly, while careening down the mountain, the relic "thudly" came to a halt. Every mechanical part was frozen. Even the lights were out. Coaxingly, she tried and retried the ignition. It wheezed, but had no power. She slid herself out of the car and, puzzled, fumbled in search of her flashlight. The night air—under a canopy of vivid stars—was beginning to chill. It could get down into the thirties, even in May, atop Haleakalā.

Suddenly, the sky lit up florescent white. She jerked her head skyward.

A glowing disc did a U-turn in the sky and headed back up the mountain leaving a windy wake. The luminescent flying object spilled over into the crater at Puʻuʻolaʻola.

"What the hell was that?" Jeannie blurted out, playing inquisitor to her own mind. "It looked like a ... " She reevaluated the vision. High altitudes can cause hallucinations. "Shee. That looked like a flying saucer!"

Jeannie was a tried-and-true UFO buff, and excitement welled up in her. She'd read all of Heinlein's pulp fiction and the serious speculations of Asimov. Her curiosity piqued. It'd only been eight years since Roswell, and Americans were still caught up in UFO fever. Of course, most UFO reportings were probably tossed pie tins, but Jeannie was not among the skeptics. She figured that with all those planets and stars up yonder, that there must be some kind of life form, oh, perhaps with three eyes and tentacles.

She hopped back into Nelliebelle. This time, the engine turned over like fine poi. She wasn't surprised. UFOlogists knew about the effects of magnetic fields. She made a U-turn on the shoulder of the road, sending rocks and gravel a couple of thousand feet down, and headed back up to the top of the crater. She passed the darkened ranger station, barreling up the snakelike blacktop that led to the overlook at Puʻuʻolaʻola, otherwise known as Red Hill. Nelliebelle screeched haphazardly to a stop in the parking lot. Jeannie ran to the overlook—an old, rock-walled bunker that perched at the edge of the gaping caldera—just in time to see the glowing disc slide into the Palikū area of the crater and disappear. She climbed atop the lava rock wall, stretched out her arms, and yelled, "I saw you!"

Suddenly she began to rise, her arms still outstretched like some redeemer, and move across the darkened terrain. She tried to scream but only a small, constipated "Ahhh" squeezed its way out. Her heart felt like it would burst, or worse. She feared that her levitation would cease and she would plummet hundreds of feet to her death. But her doubt vanished; the aliens were probably moving her with some kind of transporter power. She gleaned a cluster of silverswords, Pele's Paint Pots, and the corral where the Goddess of Fire held Kamapuaʻa, the pig god. No lights came from the three cabins spread across the miles of jet-black *pāhoehoe*. There were no humans in the crater tonight. She was the only earthling headed for Palikū at the edge of the Kīpahulu Reserve.

Slowly, she descended into the *maʻukele*. She saw the disc resting in an opening among the thickness of the *ʻōhiʻa* and *loa* trees. Things began to make sense, as she touched the ground.

This forest had always been an oddity; not only did it contain the largest collection of indigenous and rare, endangered plants in Hawaiʻi, but they were massive in size, as if they inhaled Gaviota fertilizer directly from the sky. Did this unique forest have something to do with the luminescent vehicle? Jeannie's heart was not only filled with the fear of a human tapping the unknown but also with the adrenaline rush of a reporter on top of the biggest story of her life.

A handsome Hawaiian man stepped forward from behind some massive *loa*. She guessed him to be in his late twenties, his skin bronzed smooth, his eyes showing caring mystery.

"I hope you're not afraid, Jeannie," he said. "I took this body representation from one of our previous landings. The poor young man's body was here to gather feathers for his chief. When he saw our transporter he screamed out loud that Lono had come and fell to the ground shaking. His name was Kiamanu, which you may call me, a name given to him from generations of bird catchers. I've taken his representation so that you wouldn't tremble at the site of a being different from a human."

Jeannie fumbled for her trusty notebook and grabbed her "Vote for Eddie Tam" pen.

"No need for that, Jeannie. You'll remember everything we want you to remember."

Jeannie juggled the chaos of questions in her head: Who are you? Why are you here? You came here before? Why Maui? Before the first question eeked out, the alien responded, "Who am I? Why am I here? I'll answer all those questions; then I'll have a number for you. After all, you're the only other human I've met besides the terrified bird catcher."

Jeannie added mind reading to her list of questions to the alien.

"Come inside. Come visit and get sustenance."

Doubts crossed the reporter's mind. Would she be abducted once she entered the portal and it slammed shut? Hell, she thought, the closest I ever got to a spaceship was the silly little one-seater that flashed and beeped to Little Richard records at the Maui County Fair. She thought, "I'm forty-five. What have I got to lose? Heck, maybe I'll get a Pulitzer Prize for it."

"That's the spirit, Jennie." She gulped as he pointed to the craft. The ship was as vacant as the Kahului Shopping Center on a Sunday. What it lacked in furniture, it made up for in ambience. There was a good feel to it, like a summer's day at Keawakapu Beach or a splashy waterfall in Nāhiku.

"Sit," the young man urged.

"But where?" Jeannie asked.

"Just sit and you will find your comfort."

Jeannie sat. She found herself in mid-air and shifted her body until she was comfortable. He produced, like Houdini, a blue-veined cup.

"Here, fresh, sacred water from Palihea Stream." As Jeannie sipped, the alien disguised as a Hawaiian told his tale.

"Of course, you know that Maui is a sacred place, one of several on Earth. It's one of few focus points that reach out to the Universe; Yosemite is another."

She wondered if John Muir had been visited.

"It's not only our species that has reached out to Maui. We're just one group of intergalactic voyagers."

"So you're just passing through?"

"No. We are here for a purpose. That's why we picked you—because you are willing to experiment."

He was right to some degree. She had grown up in Dayton, Ohio and, after graduation, was an intern at the *Dayton Daily News*. She listened to *Hawai'i Calls* on the radio every Sunday. The waves lapping at Waikiki lured her to visit "The Sandwich Isles." In 1950, she got the opportunity to fulfill her dream when she was assigned to cover the Daughters of the American Revolution Convention at the Royal Hawaiian Hotel.

After the convention, she returned to Dayton, threw away her winter coats, packed her cute one-piece bathing suit, and traded her position at the *Dayton Daily News* for one at the *Maui News*.

"So you picked me because I'm open-minded?"

"In part."

"What's the other part?"

"You seem to have an affinity for the species of this land."

"You mean the Hawaiian people?"

Jeannie had always tried hard to avoid being the pushy *haole* who believed she had the answers. Her Ohio parents had taught her to respect all races. The Buckeye State had been the end of the line for the Underground Railroad, and Dayton the site of the last major lynching of the Klu Klux Klan. She was determined that racism would never be part of her personal agenda.

When she arrived in Hawai'i, she got her hands on every book about Hawai'i in the Wailuku Library, and was determined to "talk story" with locals and develop a true oral history of a dwindling race. The 1950s were a crucial crossroads. The Hawaiian perspective was most needed, and Jeannie would hear their stories and feelings, and record them.

"Jeannie, what I'm asking for is a life," the alien visitor stated.

"A life?"

"We have come to this sacred place to prepare for our race's future. The planet we come from has become practically lifeless—arid and desolate from eons of feuds, jealousies, and wars. Now we have found a new place, a moving orb as beautiful as some places of your own Earth. It sits beyond the handle of what you call the Giant Dipper. We are ready to transport all our beings to this new land of three moons, sparkling vistas, breathtaking valleys like Kīpahulu, awe-inspiring mountains like Haleakalā. But we cannot go with a leader who has been tainted by greed and hostility, the very things that nearly destroyed us."

Jeannie beamed with the thought that she might go traveling to the end of the universe. What a scoop!

"Not you, Jeannie," Kiamanu interrupted. "Your fair-skinned race is on the same path of destruction as ours. You've created a deadly explosive, the atom bomb. Your war to end all wars was only the beginning."

Jeannie was upset to be put in the same cart with the white destructionists in the world. But Kiamanu was right. "Then who?" she asked.

"We want to take someone with us who is imbued with the philosophy of what these natives call Aloha, and who wants to leave their life here and help us."

Thrown by the disappointment of not being selected, Jeannie could not think of a single name, much less a list of candidates.

"Think, Jeannie. I can only receive your thoughts when you're not distracted. You've got to help me. I can't tune into the minds of the whole island. But, I understand, you're probably tired. Rest is a requirement of all active creatures. Perhaps you need some time to clear your mind of all these new, excitable impressions."

"But ... " Jeannie interjected.

"Oh, yes. Stay the night. With your sunrise, there is a new day, new beginnings, new thoughts."

"Where shall I sleep?"

"Where you are is fine. Stretch your legs, get into a comfortable position, and don't be afraid to shift in sleep. You won't fall out of the sky. Here let me create a mood for you."

With that statement, Kiamanu left, and the interior turned into a celestial womb, the sound of waves lapping on a distant shore. Jeannie tossed and turned cautiously a few times but, before she knew it, she was in a deep, peaceful slumber.

———•+•———

The sounds of birds—rare honeycreepers—whirled though Jeannie's ears. She was no longer in the craft. She stared at the pinks, lavenders, and oranges of sunrise framed by gigantic ʻōhiʻa. A waterfall splashed into a pristine pool.

"I thought you'd enjoy a normal refresher," spoke Kiamanu softly, pointing to the falls and pond.

"I knew I'd seen beautiful sunrises at Haleakalā, but this view ... "

"I agree. Our new home, the whole planet is like this."

"Eden?"

"A reference to religious beliefs?"

"Yes, Adam and Eve were the progenitors of our planet until they picked the apple."

"A story? Perhaps the apple was about inordinate power. Here." He handed her what looked like cloth.

"For wiping the water from you. I'll retreat for your modesty."

Kiamanu disappeared into the *laua'e*.

As Jeannie stepped into the cool pond, she sensed a rejuvenation, as if she had shed ten years from her fifty-year-old body. She lay back, floating in the sacred water like driftwood in space. Like that feeling after a good confession, she had been healed. As she put on her clothes, they seemed dry cleaned, devoid of all the activity of the previous day and night.

Kiamanu stepped out from behind a grand loa. He was dwarfed by the rare tree's verdant branches, the fluffy white clouds swishing across the caldera's canopy.

"Are you ready to go?" he uttered.

"Go?"

"To find our Hawaiian wise one."

"A *kupuna*? But I haven't decided …"

"Who comes to mind first?"

Jeannie was again startled. Aunty Hōkū Ka'apuni came to mind. Jeannie had spent days and nights with Aunty Hōkū in her little shack at the edge of a great expanse of taro patches in Ke'anae. They talked by her kerosene lanterns for hours about the past, her lifetime, and the stories passed down by the ancestors.

"Does she live alone?"

"She does. But … "

"How do you know that she would not like to take on the greatest challenge in her life?"

Jeannie retorted, "Well, I don't know what Aunty would think. Her husband was killed in World War I in Belgium. Her daughter was working at the commissary at Pearl Harbor on December 7, her brother hit by a bullet in the tall grass at Guadalcanal. There are no more left."

"See, war and sad stories again! Well, let's go ask her."

"But how? We'd have to drive down the mountain then take the treacherously winding roads to Keʻanae, and that would take a whole day."

"Don't worry, Jeannie. I have a transporter. We can take your car, Nelliebelle, to a convenient hideaway not far from Keʻanae and then drive into the village without being so obvious. How about the place called Seven Sacred Pools? It's isolated and right over the ridge."

"You sure you can do this?"

Kiamanu shook his head in affirmation.

"Let's go. I think you'll always remember this ride."

Kiamanu lead Jeannie back to the spaceship. As they boarded, Kiamanu coaxed Jeannie to settle in.

"We'll pick up Nelliebelle at the overlook parking lot."

"Somebody will see us." Jeannie then remembered that the Lower Kula Road would be closed for paving the day after the park dedication.

"Don't worry," said Kiamanu. "Only crazy people see flying saucers."

Jeannie chuckled in agreement. The craft hovered off of the ground and skimmed across the Palikū Plain, as Māui pulled the morning sun through Kaupō Gap.

They arrived at the overlook in moments. On an opaque visual board—an advanced version of Jeannie's Sylvania TV set at home, minus the snow—they saw Nelliebelle in the desolate parking lot, normally filled with blanket-huddled tourists from the Maui Grand Hotel.

Kiamanu somehow brought Nelliebelle into the hull of the ship. The travelers watched the screen as they zipped along the crater, up the side of the Kīpahulu Reserve and down to the pasture near the oceanside pond at Seven Sacred Pools. It, too, was deserted, feared by visitors for its potholed, winding road. The pools were a chain of lava-cooled pots that swirled and spilled the churned waters of Upper ʻOheʻo Falls one into another until they reached the sea.

Jeannie was afraid that once this pearl of nature was discovered, its sacred solitude would be lost.

"We'll take Nelliebelle into Keʻanae. No need to frighten the villagers. The craft will get there in the cover of night," explained Kiamanu, as the couple changed vehicles.

"Hop in," Jeannie urged, as they headed toward the car.

The alien slid into the side seat. "How primitive," he thought.

"By your standards," said Jeannie.

"How do you know what I was thinking?" queried Kiamanu.

"Half the humans of this planet have your gift, Kiamanu. They're called women."

He slid back in the faux leather seat and took in the tropical scenery as Nelliebelle squeaked and rattled around the snakelike turns that overlooked the blended canvass of sky and sea and jungle. Rushing waterfalls burst from the upland streams, occasionally splashing spurts onto the hood of the station wagon.

Within the hour they passed the Hasegawa General Store. They pushed through Hāna's lush lawns and, as the sun began to set, Jeannie turned down the road to the Keʻanae Peninsula. She passed the ballfield and rumbled up into the dense towering mango trees above the taro patches; a *poi* dog barked at their arrival.

"Kolohe! Nuff!" Aunty Hōkū's voice called from the verandah. The animal retreated to to the elderly woman's skirt.

"*E, nei.* Who dat? Aunty Hōkū blind these days, you know. Ass why I gotta wear dis Coke bottle glasses."

"It's me, Aunty. Jeannie!"

Aunty Hōkū giggled. "Why, I neva pay my *Maui News* last month? Nah, onee kidding, Jeannie B, come inside. I jes *pau* make fresh guava juice. The tree in back stay full. Mo bettah, yet. Sit hea on the porch. I go get um. Sit down. Sit down."

Kiamanu and Jeannie grabbed the chairs and faced them toward the ocean. Aunty Hōkū called out from the kitchen, "So who dis with you, Jeannie, your new husband?"

Kiamanu and Jeannie looked at each other. She giggled. "I wish!" she yelled back. "No, Kia is playing tourist."

Aunty Hōkū put the jiggling jelly glasses and pitcher down on the bamboo table. She studied Kiamanu, both with and without her Coke bottle glasses.

"Visitah? That's funny. You look Hawaiian. You look awfully familiar. You shua I neva met you befoa?"

"No, Aunty. He's from far away."

"Where? Calafrisco?"

"Farther."

"Boston?"

"Even farther."

Aunty Hōkū, herself, changed the topic.

"Ah, *pau nīele*. No matta where you come from, you are welcome. You guys going stay fo dinna? Almos dak. Mo bettah you stay ovanight. Dangerous."

"We were going to stay at the hotel," said Jeannie.

"Crazy! Too expensive. Only for Frank Sinatra and his gang. You stay hea."

She giggled, demanding, "An no talk back to your elders. Plus I have one nice pork belly from the church. I make kālua in da oven. Jeannie, you go cut up some tomatoes and onions and with dat and the poi, we show Kia what one autentic Hawaiian meal like."

The big question was put off until a few hours later, after the mini *lū'au* was joyfully consumed, the dishes washed, wiped, and stacked on the rack. The stars glistened. Kiamanu stared at a particular one.

"You stare at that star like it's your home, Kia," said Aunty as she placed a cup of coffee for him on the table on the verandah. "Ass the Hōkūle'a there at the end of the handle of the dippa. The star that guided our ancestors here."

"Our new home is just beyond that, " Kia confessed, the quivering of the lamplight playing on his face.

"I love coming to Aunty's house," interjected Jeannie, returning from the bathroom. "No electricity as you notice. Everything's the basics."

"So, Jeannie, what brought you to Ke'anae. Nothing happening in town?" asked the kupuna.

"Kia wants to ask you a question."

"Go ahead, Kia. I dunno if I can answer the $64,000 Question, I only went to sophomore yea at Lahainaluna, but I try."

Kia proceeded. "Aunty, did you ever wonder at the significance of your name?"

"I have. True Hawaiians are usually named after some good omen sensed at the time of birth. My mākuahine named me 'traveling star.' My mother strangely added that my name would be fulfilled in the future. I laugh at the thought of traveling star when I have been in this little house at the edge of the taro patch for over sixty years. Most think I dead."

Kia stretched out and held her hand. "Well, Aunty, I believe that it's time to explore your name."

As the oil lamps continued to throw flickered images onto the aged hut's walls, Kiamanu told Aunty who he was and about his people. He told her about the mean and warlike inhabitants of his world who had destroyed their homeland and that a diaspora had finally found a hospitable and inviting planet."

Aunty was riveted and moved by the story. "But I still don't see why you're here at my humble hale."

Kiamanu was straightforward. "You, Aunty, whether you believe it or not, are the embodiment of a philosophy of love. You call it aloha. We want you to be our wise one, our counselor."

"A kupuna?" asked Aunty. "All kupuna should have some wisdom from a life of experience, but I'm at the end of my life, Kia. What good could an old lady like me provide?"

"Years of goodness, decades of love."

Aunty Hōkū pondered the implications deeply in silence so quiet that all could hear, in the distance, the breakers pounding on the ebony shards of lava along the shoreline.

Kiamanu added, after a pause, "Plus, if you were to go with us, the travel would actually reverse the aging process. Not too many earthlings get a second chance."

Aunty Hōkū walked to the edge of the porch and stared out at Hōkūleʻa and beyond. "There are so many pains and sorrows on this earth. But there is also so much good that I know I'd miss—the sunrise showering down on Haleakalā, purple sunsets, the winds grazing the tops of the leaves in the loʻi, the squeals of children coming from the ball field."

She suddenly turned and said, with a voice of harsh reality, "But all these would, anyway, be gone in a year or two or three at the most. At ninety-two, where I going but die?"

A sense of sadness was felt by all.

"Your memory of these things will not be forgotten in your next life," said Kiamanu, supportively.

"Then, we go!" blurted Aunty Hōkū. "Let's fulfill the prophecy and go star traveling. Let's make Mama happy."

A tear dropped down from Jeannie's face. Even she, with all her curiosity about life, would take pause at such a serious decision.

"What do I need to take?" she asked Kiamanu.

"What you want," he replied.

Aunty Hōkū retreated to the bedroom. Jeannie and Kiamanu stared at each other. The elderly woman returned with a *lauhala* bag and suitcase. She giggled, twirling around, "Do you think they'll like my *muʻumuʻu?*"

"Fashionable. But so little to take?" asked Jeannie.

"All up here," said Aunty pointing to her head. "Kolohe!" she called the dog, and he scampered in. She petted him down one final time.

"You take care of Jeannie, Kolohe."

He gave a look of understanding. She took some paper from the old desk and began writing. "I'll leave a paper, Jeannie, granting this house and land to the church for whatever they want."

When all was done, Aunty locked the house and handed Jeannie the key and kissed her. "What? We going into space in Nelliebelle?"

Jeannie laughed.

"Your carriage, Aunty, awaits you at the ball field."

The craft was sitting, waiting on the large lawn, transported there from ʻOheʻo. Jeannie and Aunty Hōkū hugged each other once more.

"Thank you, Jeannie for helping my people," said Aunty.

"And mine too, Jeannie," added Kiamanu. He outstretched his arms around her and came close to a human blush. "I like this feeling of aloha!" Then he made his way up the ramp and entered the ship.

"Maybe someday, Jeannie, I'll return to see you and tell you all about my great adventure," Aunty called out. They both began to tear. "Nuff! The kupuna got work to do."

Later, Jeannie swore that when Aunty Hōkū turned back for one last glance, she had already begun to lose the lines of experience that crossed her face; her carriage upright, that of a younger, proud Hawaiian woman.

Jeannie stood with Kolohe in the dark as the disc hurtled upward into the inky night toward the archipelago of stars in the south. Kolohe barked a final farewell, scampered up to Nelliebelle, and hopped in the front seat as if to say, "Well, Jeannie, what you waiting for?"

Jeannie was glad it would take hours to get to Wailuku. She would need the time to reflect on the many wonders she had just experienced, while driving along the winding road from Keʻanae.

Luahinepiʻi
The Climbing Woman

Luahinepiʻi: Ka Wahine Piʻina

A WHITE LADY STORY

It was all part of the ritual among the boys. They had been at it for years. The object was simple: scare the hell out of the girls! Suspension of disbelief is essential to horror fantasies, and the boys knew that the girls were as good as acting frightened as the boys were in playing evil maniacs who could jump out of bushes and chase the fair maidens for yards.

The guys had honed in on their paranormal mischief from their weekly Sunday attendance at the *King Theater* that featured cheesy B horror movies from American International in black and white. Of course, the girls were victims of psychotic maniacs so often that they would have felt disappointed if they hadn't been the target of an elaborate hoax the next week.

The *modus operandi* to scare the girls was, for the boys, to alternate the responsibilities of "Monster of the Week" to keep the girls thinking. The object was also to rotate the locations of the encounters. At this time, in the early '60s, Maui was still quite rural. There were so many spooky sites to perform these mini-productions: valleys, beaches, and forests that were still untouched by coming developments.

Tonight was Leslie's chance. First, there was the alibi as to why he wouldn't make it to the big St. Anthony-Baldwin High game.

His grandmother was sick. Agnes and Bill were out of town and Leslie had to take care of his ailing Nana. The girls were already suspicious of his excuse, made earlier that day, as they waved their pom poms on what would again be a lopsided victory. For one thing, Leslie's grandmother (Nana) had died twenty-five years earlier. Secondly, Aggie and Bill had been seen by one of the girls buying poki at Nagasako Fish Market that very morning.

The White Lady story had been passed down from earlier generations. She was said to have appeared in ʻĪao and Waiheʻe Valleys as well as along the road to Hāna. No one could pinpoint the rationale behind her appearances. Was she Pele? But Pele wore red and did not appear in the folklore of these Maui locations.

Even Old Man Costa, who had lived in ʻĪao Valley when it was a series of taro patches, claims to have talked to The White Lady. He professed to have seen her in the midst of the kukui forest drying her gossamer-like dresses. He said that she was not Hawaiian, but, true to her moniker, white! His wife claimed that he had been drinking ʻōkolehao heavily during that period and that the mystery woman was probably a pre-hippy who was living off the fertile land above Wailuku.

Tonight, Leslie would be part of the White Lady performance. He had snatched from the school's moldy costume room a stringy white wig that had been used by the witch in a past Spring Festival production of *Hansel and Gretel*. Even Leslie's sister Blanche had gotten in on the act by sewing a flowing *lava lava* and kīhei to fit his boyish body.

Luckily, he had kept a stash of greases and paints from past Halloweens. He would apply it to his entire body to make sure there was no doubt that this was, indeed, The White Lady. The homecoming game would probably be out by nine. The gang would first head over to Shirley's for some burgers and cokes. Then, one of the boys, as credibly as he could, would suggest, "Hey, let's go up ʻĪao Valley tonight."

One of the girls protested that there was no moon and that it would be dangerous running through the valley on the darkest of nights. After all, someone could get hurt. After a few clucking sounds by the boys attributed to her lack of guts, the play-along girls re-initiated their bravado and agreed to the great adventure. In their minds, however, was the demand, "This better be a damn good show!"

At about halftime, Leslie packed his wardrobe, makeup, and the plywood ax he'd made in Cub Scouts into his Valiant and headed up the valley. He would change and apply the makeup and eventually find a good hiding place down by the stream, where he knew the girls would be taken. He would let the "victims" pass him and then "terrorize" them. With no outlet, they would run off the beaten path deeper into the inky forest.

The valley was as quiet as death when Leslie arrived. He parked his car down in Kepaniwai Park, hidden so the girls wouldn't see it. The guest monster then walked up the winding road toward the Needle, a 1,200-foot phalanx that protruded from the now extinct volcano. Les knew that the Needle and the caldera were more than geographical phenomena. They were steeped in legend in the stories of the Valley Isle. The Needle was Puʻuokamoa, the merman, who fell in love with ʻĪao, the daughter of Maui and Hina, when they lived in the sacred place.

ʻĪao had been forbidden by her father to continue her love affair with the man who lived in the stream that cut through land. She ignored her father and, when he caught her, he asked if she wanted to see Puʻuokamoa forever. She agreed, and her father transformed Puʻuokamoa into rock, the Needle that ʻĪao, sadly, had agreed to see forever.

He also knew that this was the valley Hiʻiaka had visited on her way to fetch Lohiaʻu for her sister, Pele. The Aliʻi Nui of the valley was an insensitive ogre who refused to meet with Hiʻiaka, much less share aloha with food and lodging. In retaliation, she flung the king's body all the way to Waiheʻe, his bones imbedded into the cliffsides of that valley.

But Leslie doubted the White Lady story. He presumed that it had been concocted by fathers and grandfathers for years perhaps to keep truant boys from late-night adventures. Still, as Leslie squatted in the bushes, an uneasiness came over him. Perhaps it was the dead silence. Perhaps it was the wind that occasionally rattled the leaves. Perhaps it was the sudden, unrhythmic splash in the stream. He thought he heard chanting in the distance from Camp Dole, burned down by some anti-Hawaiians after Liliuʻokalani had visited there.

He looked in that direction. His mind stopped the chanting. All he could see in the distance were the lights of Wailuku peeking through the gap in the valley. Then he heard, in back of him, a voice, a voice that sounded like it came from cracked record played at the wrong speed. He couldn't believe what he saw. A woman in white made her way up the path, perhaps a joke by one of the other boys? Months later, remembering a few key words, he'd find out from his old Hawaiian uncle the meaning of what she kept repeating: *"Ua lohe ʻia ka leo kapū e ke ipo i moealoha."*

His heart beat like a pounding *pahu*. She was headed his way. Like any normal human being, he got up and ran like hell—up the steep embankment—looking back every few steps to notice that he was not shaking her away.

Leslie's silly witch's wig was snagged by a protruding guava branch, and he ran hairless into the night. The lava lava started to slip, exposing his BVDs. The malo dropped to his ankles. He lost his balance up the incline and tripped. He rolled downhill onto some large boulders that bordered the stream just under the long bridge that traversed it. He passed out.

Water dripped onto his face. Leslie could hear the placid stream again. He was relieved that he was among the living. Or so he thought. He looked straight ahead and felt secure that he had survived that silly fall caused by his sense of overimagination about a white lady and all that jazz…

"You made fun of me."

He turned suddenly to find that his nightmare was not over. There, seated on a boulder, was the White Lady. She repeated the complaint, "You made fun of me."

"I'm sorry," Leslie replied, confused. "I … I thought you were just made up."

She responded with the gravel voice.

"Just because you don't know history doesn't mean I never existed. Those who are alive foolishly believe that things only exist within their short passage through this life."

Although he was repulsed by her atrocious voice, he finally noticed, with the clearing of his head, that she was extremely beautiful, not like the old-hag ghosts from the movies. Curiously, he asked her for a name.

"My name is Luahinepi'i."

His limited knowledge of Hawaiian, limited to short phrases and foods, was of no help.

"What does it mean?

"It means Old Woman."

He was confused. She was young and beautiful. Perhaps it had to do with her harsh voice.

"To dispel your ignorance, I will share with you what very few know—my story."

As she said this, Leslie became more aware of the sounds of the stream that split the valley at the point where the rickety wooden bridge spanned it. The sounds began to lull him and, like a liquid mantra, cast him into a hypnotic state. He leaned his head against a boulder and fell into a coma.

A sound of a baby crying woke him. He was no longer in 'Īao. He was in a hut of pili grass. A woman reposed on layers of leaf and kapa holding the crying baby at her breast. A male hovered over her, concerned.

"Where am I?" asked Leslie.

No one responded, perhaps busy with the concern of birth at hand. He tried the question again. They acted as if he wasn't there. He moved to the puka and looked out. He recognized it as *Paukūkalo*; his aunty Mary had a house *makai* of the road. But there were no wooden houses, just a series of grass huts. He had gone back in time.

The baby cried again, the voice agitated, like *'ili 'ili* rolling at the ocean's edge. The parents gave looks of concern. *"Wa'u, Wa'u!"* they repeated over and over again. Although he was not fluent in Hawaiian, he understood every word. "Grating, Grating!" it was said of something being scraped. Leslie moved in closer to the child, aware that, despite his closeness to the couple, they were oblivious to their visitor from the future. He looked at the child—a beautiful girl.

The parents wrapped the child in kapa and headed for the *heiau* for her blessing. As Leslie left the hut to follow them, he noticed something strange. The clouds zipped by, the sun and moon alternating in the heavens like a movie scene where time passes by.

A young girl in her teens raced toward the hut. Leslie recognized her eyes as the eyes of the crying baby. Her eyes were still filled with tears. Behind her followed girls of her age taunting her with epithets: "Coconut shredding 'opihi! Lava scraper! Clawing Boar!"

Her father, hearing the slurs, rushed to the *hale puka* and yelled at them, *"Hele ma kahi 'e!"* The teens scattered. Luahinepi'i rushed into her father's arms. From their conversation, Leslie found out that this was not the first time that cruelty had been hurled at his daughter. Her father assured her that she was beautiful and the girls were simply jealous so they had to make fun of her voice.

He only wished that her mother were still alive to give her the comfort that only a mother can give. He emphasized that her voice was *akua*-given and that she should accept the fate the gods had given her. But her father's consolation could not erase the hurt she felt. Her depression was somewhat relieved by long walks up from the mouth of the stream deep into the forests of ʻĪao Valley.

Leslie followed her on some of these walks. No one doubted the therapeutic benefits of such hikes on most human beings. The tranquility of the ʻāina would have soothed the souls of the normally troubled. But Luahinepiʻi's sojourns seemed to aggravate her hurt. The valley, as all the natives knew, was more often cloudy than sunny, so the sable clouds further scarred her state of sadness.

Suddenly Luahinepiʻi's life took a change for the better. Someone new moved into Paukūkalo. His name was *Manaʻolaula*, a Hilo boy whose mother had returned to her home village by the sea after his father had drowned on a fishing trip. She had noticed him at a *hukilau* one night, surrounded by young girls who were drawn to his charm and looks.

She noticed his rippling muscles as he tugged at the net. He glanced at her with his ebony eyes but she shook it off. He might be initially interested in her but all would end when he heard her voice. A week passed. One day, Luahinepiʻi went mountainside to pick *lauwaʻe*. As she passed a pond, she noticed a naked body dash from the water to a nearby clump of mountain apple trees. A malo was grabbed from a branch of the *kaumani* tree that shaded the pool; ebony eyes peeked from behind the grove, laughing.

"Sorry. I didn't know anyone else was around."

It was Manaʻolaula. Luahinepiʻi was pleasantly surprised at the chance visit. She giggled shyly.

"And you are Luahinepiʻi," he pronounced.

"How do you know my name?"

"Paukūkalo village is as small as Hilo."

"I must go."

She gathered up the *lauwaʻe* and turned.

"Don't go!"

"I have to. I must prepare tonight's meal," she insisted.

"The sun has only a short time ago passed toward afternoon. There is plenty time to prepare for only two of you."

"How do…?" She halted mid-sentence, aware of the intimacy of a village.

"Come sit on these rocks while I continue my interrupted swim."

"Oh, don't feel sorry. Are you up for a swim too?"

"Single men usually don't swim with women," she insisted.

"When no one is around, there is none to accuse," he retorted. And in one movement, Mana'olaula, tore off the malo and dove into the placid pool.

"Come on, Luahinepi'i. I'll turn the other way."

His twelve-hand spanned frame turned away, the young woman paying attention to the detail of running droplets of water glistening as it flowed down his back. Leslie felt uncomfortable watching, but became immediately aware of the blossoming love of the two.

Luahinepi'i slid into the pond. Days went by; meetings were discreet. But Mana'olaula never spoke of the raspy voice of Luahinepi'i. She became more and more puzzled about it.

Other boys of her age had been as insensitive as the jealousies of the gossipy girls. Attracted first by her beauty, they coiled repulsively at her first pronouncement. She waited for a day to bring the question up. He invited her to walk along the sand dunes of lower Waiehu. Leslie followed the couple and listened in.

The trades were blowing softly and Haleakalā stood clear in the distance. She had brought along some *kūlolo* to nibble at and found a flat area above the dunes for sitting. After some talk of the beauty of the area, Luahinepi'i asked the big question.

"Mana'olaula?"

"Yes?"

"I'm curious. You haven't mentioned anything about my voice. I was wondering why?"

"I had a very wise father."

"I'm sorry. I heard that he died while fishing."

"A rogue wave suddenly came out of nowhere and overturned the canoe. The outrigger hit his head and he began to sink. When his fishing friend pulled him up, it was already too late. His breath had left him."

"I'm sorry."

"We cannot undo what has been done. That's one important thing I learned from his advice and his death. Now you know why I have not reacted to your voice. Oh, I'm not crazy; I hear the same voice as others hear, but the gods, not you or your father or your mother, caused this. The only thing we can do about our flaws is to accept them."

"I understand. I wish others would."

"Lack of understanding is their flaw. They will just have to face it in the future. But there's more than that flaw, Luahinepi'i. The rest of you is so full of love and kindness. And your beauty ... ? You're fairer than the *Lokelani*. What more is there?"

Luahinepi'i blushed naturally. She almost couldn't believe what she heard. Everything about her voice had been negative. Even if it were true, haunting doubts plagued her. It would be hard just to forget all the negativity in one day on a bluff watching the rain clouds skip over Pā'ia.

Unfortunately, Mana'olaula's *tūtūwahine*, aged ninety-five, was coming to the end of her life. Her husband and sons were long gone and so the responsibility fell to the eldest grandson. Mana'olaula set sail to Hilo to take care of her in her final days.

When he told Luahinepi'i, she immediately fell into a gloom. Without him, she felt vulnerable and subject to the taunting of vicious girls. Days passed and Mana'olaula's grandmother continued to hold on physically. Her days in the lo'i had made her strong in body despite increasing confusion. The wicked gossips of Paukūkalo took advantage of the situation to begin rumors that Mana'olaula had not only returned to Hilo but to his former lover as well.

Luahinepiʻi, separated by ocean, conjured up images of betrayal in spite of the fact that she knew they were fabrications of jealous women. Leslie felt her hurt. From that day on, Luahinepiʻi would only wear white as a sign of waiting for her lover to return.

Two full moons came and went. Luahinepiʻi fell into a darker time. She didn't know who to believe. One of the destroyers of reputation, Hoʻolapa returned from Hilo. A fellow member of Luahinepiʻi's hula troupe, she felt wickedly obliged to set Luahinepiʻi straight.

Leslie watched from the window.

"Luahinepiʻi!" Hoʻolapa called from outside the sad one's hale.

Luahinepiʻi came to the puka. Noting her as one of the uncontrolled tongues of the village, she snapped back, "What do you want?"

"I've just returned from Hilo with news of Manaʻolaula."

"It can't be good news coming from your mouth," she muttered.

"I just wanted you to know so you wouldn't be hurt."

Luahinepiʻi ground her teeth at the statement. "Ignorant," she said to herself, "of all the previous hurt, you crab." Then out loud, "Well, let's get straight to the point. What did you see him do?"

"It's not only what I saw; it's also what I heard."

"Heard?"

"He's been seen around Hilo with a woman of his age. Some say she is as beautiful as the rainbows above the Wailuku River. I didn't want to leap to a conclusion. After all, she could be a cousin. But one night, a few of us girls were returning from a day at the beach. The moon was already up and we were in an especially good mood having met a man with some strong *ʻōkolehau*. As we approached Manaʻolaula's compound, we heard the sounds of lovemaking coming from the hale. How he could do that there with his tūtūwahine fading away in another area disturbed us."

Luahinepiʻi kept repeating in her mind over and over as the story unfolded, "Liar, Liar. Manaʻolaula loves me!"

"But that's not all," Hoʻolapa continued. Luahinepiʻi's heart sank. "He accidentally called out your name in the act of love."

The gossip started to leave, but turned.

"I thought it best that you know that he is not a true lover. It's best to know before you get hurt." She turned and walked away.

"Before you get hurt? What about getting hurt now?!" the young girl cried out.

Hopelessness shadowed her mind. Unstoppable tears flowed. Luahinepiʻi raced from the *hale* and up along the path into ʻĪao Valley. She ran and collapsed on the dirt trail. The girl with the gravelly voice picked herself up and continued on, talking to herself, letting the sordid scene play over and over again. She spiraled downward in her misery. Clouds initially dropped small tears from the heavens to commiserate with her. Then, blackened billows began to gather up beyond Puʻuokamoa.

Now it was pouring heavily, but the depressed woman was oblivious to it. She pressed on, slipping occasionally into the puddles that were forming. Small streams spilled off the cliffsides onto the path. Finally, Luahinepiʻi spotted the place that would end this misery. It was a steep climb up to the ledge that would take her out of her suffering.

Lightning flashed in the distance. In her mind the gods were telling her that this was the right decision. She clawed her way, higher and higher, slipping occasionally, slamming her knees against the cruel rocks. She groped at sharp lava shards that sliced her palms, the blood comingling with the rainwater that poured from the precipices above. She was oblivious to these pains; they were minor to the larger dolor that ripped at her heart.

When Luahinepiʻi reached the top of the ledge, everything stopped. She gazed up and down the weeping valley. Exhausted, she faced the thought that she would be home soon. She would be with her mother and ancestors. As the rain resumed, Luahinepiʻi raised her arms to the heavens and leaped; her body hurtled several hundred feet down onto a canopy of quivering kukui leaves and then onto the boulders alongside the ʻĪao Stream.

A trickle of water flowed down Leslie's face.

"Leslie?" The teen opened his eyes to the woman standing over him. "Are you good? I know that not everyone gets to relive another's life. But, perhaps, you will understand more than others." She started to retreat back down towards the stream from which she came.

"Luahinepiʻi?" he called out after her.

"Yes?"

"Like ghosts, you have to tell me why you still continue to be here."

"Ghost? I am not a ghost. I do not haunt. I do not scare. I am just a sad woman who waits for her lover to come back from Hilo. When Manaʻolaula returns, he will tell me the truth; then we will live happily together."

NOTES ON SHORT STORIES

*Here are some pre-thoughts and after-thoughts
on each of the stories.*

Under Maui Skies

When I first set out to write a Western set on Maui, I was doubtful I'd find an interesting yarn. After all, Maui was not the Old West; it was too laid back. I wasn't aware of mainland-style cattle rustling, bank robberies, or showdowns at noon. This, I thought, would be a challenge. I met with two old-timers who had worked at Haleakalā Ranch and other small Upcountry operations. Paniolo veterans David Ventura, Sr., and Henry Silva were exciting sources of the life of the paniolo and their nemeses. They claimed that Albert Devil, the antagonist of "Under Maui Skies", was a real person. At first I was skeptical, but after being reminded that this island has a cast of characters with story associated names like "Two Fingers Cabral" and "Carburetor Medeiros," I took their word that the man in black was for real. I picked the title "Under Maui Skies" from the style of one of many Roy Rogers and Gene Autry Westerns produced by Republic Pictures in the 1930s and '40s, and set the story against the background of the 1908 success of ʻIkuā Purdy at the Cheyenne Rodeo Nationals. I ended the story in a comic vein but, in reality, Albert Devil killed the person who stiffed him. The body was found several months later in one of the area's lava tubes.

The Cave of Whispering Spirits

I was curious about the last eruption of Haleakalā and went nīele to find out any stories associated with it. The stories I was able to discover, familiar to some Hawaiians, had the makings of a natural Adventure Story. Interestingly enough, the date of the eruption that helped create La Perouse Bay had been estimated to have occurred in 1790, but recent carbon dating now tells us that it was a hundred years earlier. I blended two stories. One is of the young lovers Paea and Kalua, who failed to recognize and help Pele when she visited them. The other is about a family who raised chickens to offer a feast to Pele when she came. In both cases, insensitivity blinded them from the requests of the Fire Godess. As a result, the singular beauty of a once, long sandy bay was overrun by Pele, the punished characters now embedded as lava features in Honuaʻula. Sadly, as I wrote this, Maui was battling against a proposed development in the area of 700 luxury homes—a development that would silence the Cave of Whispering Spirits.

The Cruel Sun

When I considered the Love Story genre, I turned to something I knew little about—Princess Nāhiʻenaʻena and Prince Kauikeaouli. I had written about many of the figures of the monarchy in my plays *Children of the Turning Tide* and *Only the Morning Star Knows*, but had never dealt with this young couple. Students of Hawaiian history know generally of their bloodline affair and their condemnation by the missionaries. But, I thought, "What if some readers didn't know about the brother-and-sister relationship? Would they still support their partnership of love once they found out? Would they retain their Western bias or would they accept their relationship in the context of time and culture? I took the license of misdirection and plunged the reader—*in media res*—into the couple's throes of love. Part of this misdirection was created by giving Nāhiʻenaʻena her Christian name, Harriet, the baptismal name given to her by her mother, Keōpūolani. Kaui, of course, is short for Kauikeaouli. There were few documents about the couple, and those were dry narratives merely of what took place. In this story, as author, I could provide a chance for readers to listen in on their affections, their dreams, and battles with personal demons and missionaries. If I've caught you up in the love shared by these two, then I will have succeeded as a writer.

Aloha, Sweetheart

Aloha ʻoe, e Kuʻu Ipo is, of course, an homage to the Detective genre, specifically the California writers Dashell Hammet and Raymond Chandler. Their heroes, like Sam Spade and Philip Marlowe, were paycheck-to-paycheck private eyes who bungled their ways in and out of crime. Their jaded views of humanity came out of the disillusions of post-World War I. Although thousands of miles apart, these case-desperate dreamers share many things in common with their Hawaiian counterparts: The kona winds parallel L.A.'s Santa Ana winds; Leilani Lau is similar to every obviously guilty femme fatale who ever sauntered into a private dick's disheveled office; and Kats, Simplicio, and Patsy are counterparts to the bevy of losers like the movies' Peter Lorre, Elisha Cook Jr., and Sydney Greenstreet. An interested producer suggested a film version, so a script was produced. The challenge was to translate a nine-page story into a seventy-five-page script. While some of the short story murder evidence is gathered off-page, the screenplay allows a wider scope. In the film version, we follow Tony and Tedo, his Puerto Rican teenage partner, in their search for proof. Included is every director's dream scene—a chase down Haleakalā in 1930s' automobiles. The project is, in show biz parlance, in pre-production.

Aunty Becky's Tavern

For the Military/War genre, I decided to follow the wartime footsteps of my father. After his death, I realized that I had never talked to him seriously about his service at Guadalcanal. I understood, of course, that this was part of the consistent silence of members of the armed services that many families experience. Their husbands, fathers, and sons avoided discussion of the horrors of war. Even though

I could follow my father's troop movement to the Solomons through wartime documents and books, what was missing were the guts of his experience. All the stories in this book come from a thumbnail sketch of events. Lacking were the inner thoughts and conversations that can only be filled in by calling upon, through imagination, the spirits of these people. The setting and title is *Aunty Becky's Tavern*, Kihei's only watering hole that existed across from Kalama Park until the late 1960s. There, in a *Twilight Zone* world, Val confronts the horrors of war and its lasting effects.

An Island Beyond Hōkūle'a

The Science Fiction genre would be my greatest, and most rewarding, challenge. Most of my plays and stories have been based on true stories. Here I had to rely entirely on imagination and, at the same time, make the story as believable as possible. Not many Hawaiian works merge with outer-space stories. Luckily, I have been a fan of Isaac Asimov, Robert Heinlein, and Arthur C. Clarke. In this story, I wanted to achieve the same feelings that Clarke evoked in his novel *Childhood's End*. Instead of children leaving earth, old people would go. The story eventually evolved to Aunty Hōkū fulfilling her lifelong destiny to take the philosophy of aloha to a new world—the island beyond Hōkūle'a. It was only natural that Haleakalā would be the setting, with a focus on Palikū. It has been rumored for years that Haleakalā is a special place on earth, a portal to parallel universes. The character that holds the story together, Jeannie Booth, is based on Jeannie Booth Johnson, a *Maui News* reporter of the period who was not afraid to discuss her sightings and interest in ufology.

Luahinepi'i: The Climbing Woman

For the Ghost Story, something obvious came to mind—the White Lady. For years, Mauians have heard of the White Lady of ʻĪao. Where had this story come from? Who was the White Lady? Was she real or was it "a tale made up by mothers and fathers to keep young boys at home and in their beds?" I started my usual research procedures and came across a snippet talking about the story of Luahinepi'i, "The Climbing Woman." With a mere five sentences of a plotline, I fleshed a more complete story of the girl with the grating voice. As boys, we had exploited the story of The White Lady to the point that we actually created little dramas to scare our female teenage companions. One of these scenarios appears in my play *Under the Star of Gladness*. Like a scene from the drama, the short story starts in the 1960s, when Leslie, the teenage main character, is confronted by the spirit of a woman who climbed up one of the precipices to commit suicide. Leslie is taken back in time to pre-contact Hawaiʻi, where he witnesses the story, from birth to tragic death, of Luahinepi'i, the ghostly woman who wanders ʻĪao waiting for her lover to return.

KAONA AND
OTHER MELE

The Roselani
Ka Roselani

Fair grows the rose
Of Wahikuli
Fragile petals
Protected from the sweltering noon
in the shade of tall mango trees
And the clouds that skim off of the uplands.
Unobtrusive, her fragrance.
West winds blow her seeds over the mountain
Onto Puʻu Hale Nani.
The same clouds that sheltered her at Wahikuli
Now protect her in Wailuku.
Without the heat of the cruel sun,
She flourishes.
Her shrub bountiful with children
Blushed by the morning blessings of Haleakalā.
They inherit her soft barbs.
She stands in the forefront of a meandering stream
A complexion of pink innocence
Adding more beauty to an already beautiful world.

The Night-Blooming Cereus

Ka Pānini o ka Puna Hou

O Special Flower
 Your arrival
Foreshadowed by perfume
The summer night warm
The moon full
The splashes in the waterway
Stilled
Everything sensitive to your bloom
Rare magnificence
The glory of life
No matter how short
The matter how worthwhile
A double corona of yellow and white
Transforming the rock wall
Mottled by a million stars
And as the morning Hongwanji bells
Beat out slow, then fast, then faster
She starts to close
Her sensual beauty gone
Only memories now as we wait
Wait to see her bloom again.

The White Ginger of California

Ka 'Awapuhi Ke'oke'o o Kaleponi

Driftwood descendant

Across the Pacific

The flower slip grows

Under the mountain's view

Where bowers of flowers bloom in the sun.

The child of Pā'ia

She evades the cold winds of winter

And thrives

Among the Agapantha

Like the blue of the 'uki 'uki berry

Of her homeland.

Three buds blossom

In white purity.

Your perfume sanctifies the other plants

Sweet Scent of Heaven.

Tell the refrain

Of the white ginger of California.

Although out of their habitat, some of Hawai'i's indigenous plants and flowers continue to live a life of aloha in other places. In Northern and Southern California, for example, slips of white ginger and variations of the flower survive and thrive, under the care of transplanted native Hawaiians.

The Mango

Ka Manakō

———·•·———

Hard to reach
That red-orange-golden one
That shines above the canopy
Haloed by the rays of Haleakalā.
It's been there, ripening
Forbidden, even to the birds.
Others have dropped to the ground
They repose in the pili grass
Covered by spray of morning dew.
Others are spotted
Too soft
Her flowers, unique, with red hairs
And now, summer has come.
It's time.
The Grower approaches
Tenderly climbing the branched steps
Delicately he plucks
Carries down like Hiʻiaka at the breast of Pele
Close to his bosom
Only a young one with a pure heart
With juices dripping
Will enjoy the mango.

The Bougainvillea

Ka Pukanawila

Blushed
like the sunsets
poked by the jagged peaks
of the West Maui Mountains.
She could have been white, red, purple,
But she is crimson,
The color of passion and pain.
A shoot once,
A thriving bush now,
Her full bracts
A tribute to beauty.
Thorns bar her core.
Her paper petals fall in the heat,
A carpet created under her shade
For the weary not to worry.
The flower, that decorated Madeira's cliffs
and Wailuku's Valley of Kukui,
Adorns the coal ground,
Now dreams the memories of a nourishing ʻĪao.

The Cherry Blossom
Ka Pua Keli

———•••———

O fair flower
Announcer of the spring
Beautiful indeed is the cherry blossom.
Budding
Opening
And blossoming
Her colors brighten life
The flower that attracts
Surrounded by her flower family.
A blossom on the top most branch
Tiny is the flower yet it scents the surrounding grasses.
Unfolded by the water is the face of the flower.
She flutters down into the stream
After her glory
She floats to her Source.

The cherry blossom is not an indigenous flower of Hawai'i but has a strong connection to the Japanese community. It is one symbol in the bouquet of people who populate Hawai'i Nei.

The Ten-Cent Flower
Ka Puakenikeni Nui

—··—

Oh, unique plant
Her blossoms bigger than the other *puakenikeni*
Large to contain the unending aloha of her homeland—Maui.
Nourished by the fine, misty rains of the West Maui Mountains
Twelve men tall
She protects the life beneath.
Three periods of a short but colorful life:
First day—white—the white
of billowy clouds over Puʻu Kukui
Second day—yellow—
the yellow of the dawn of Haleakalā
Third day—orange—
Like the orange sunset off Lahaina.
Her flowers blossom in the evening
Perfumed twilight
Fragrant flower of the night
Her soft scent wins the heart.
The puakenikeni is twisted
Entwined by the *maile*
Embraced by the tuberose and *koa*.
When you water that flower
Fondly remember the song
Of the grand puakenikeni.

In ʻĪao Valley, and only on Maui grows a unique puakenikeni tree, her flowers twice the size of the standard puakenikeni. The tree stands forty feet tall and has a canopy of thirty feet; its location silent on the lips of those determined to preserve its past and future.

The Shooting Star

Ka Hōkū Welowelo

You came quickly
A shooting star
In the night
I noticed you, shining
But I paid more attention
To others' needs
And when I looked back
You were gone.
I was foolish
To have not spent more time enjoying you.
You will return
Within a lifetime
Like the star of the child named Paiʻea.
Let the story be told of
The Shooting Star
I saw your shining beauty.
Come back!

A Pink Spiral Cloud

Ka Ao 'Ākala Mo'oni

A pink spiral cloud
Appears over Waiehu
Unique
In contrast
To Haleakalā's blue.
A puffy top
The color of the *roselani*
A joyful toy
Hovering over
The sky's mirror.
When dark clouds invade
Let the refrain be told
Of the pink spiral cloud.

In the ancient days of Hawai'i, a baby's first birthday was celebrated. The boy or girl had passed a crucial period without illness. This was another occasion to write a kaona.

A Child Lei

He Lei Kamali‘i

A beloved one
Fondled in the arms
Carried on the back
Arms around the neck like a lei
A lei never forgotten is the child.

A summer lei,
A winter lei,
Is the child.

Steadfast like the Pīlali gum sticks to the kukui
Inviting like the sea scent of Wai‘ehu
Sweet like the taro of Ke‘anae

A lei that is never set aside
is one's child.

The Lehua of Hawai'i Island

Ka Lehua O Hawai'i Nui

The skies cried
Its own precious flower was picked
Separated from her branch
Pele loved the *'ōhi'a* too late
She shook her stamen
Annointing the forest with honey dew
She came from the lone *lehua* of Ka'ala
An attractive flower on the upmost branch
She came from a tree covered with birds
A tolerant towering evergreen
Thriving in the cloud forest
Clinging along the ocean edge at Nāpō'opo'o
Her reflection in a fresh water pond of Waimea
Those far from Hawai'i
Inhaled the lehua mixed with *maile* and *hala*
The precious lover of heaven
Now adorns the altar of Laka.
Let the refrain be told
A soft hymn
of the golden lehua o *Hawai'i Nui.*

The Sands of Our Beautiful Hill Home

Ke One o Ka Puʻu Hale Nani

Famous are the sands of Ewa, Puna, Waimea, and Nohili
But none like the sand of our beautiful hill home
Sacred is this sand
Overlooking the ʻŌmaʻomaʻo Plain
Cool in the shade of the West Maui Mountains
Firm is this sand
Each grain important; each dependent on the other
Fine and peaceful is this sand
You sparkle under the blue of sky and the gold of sun
Thank you, O Creator for our homeland
Tell again about
The Sands of Our Beautiful Hill Home.

Ka Mahina Loke
Rose Moon

Blushed moon
Lokelani hued
Seemingly sitting still in the western sky
Frame: Lace fringed delicate billows.
Oh, gently coaxed crescent
You travel your arched path
Across the studded inky vastness.
Jupiter joins you,
And two glittered companions
Bask in your light.
Your beam illuminates
Cleggan,
The Headlands of Marin
And Maui's head,
Simultaneously, from this spot on a strand of sand at Kihei.
Soon she outraces her stellar partners;
She duplicates the rose lei pattern of a multitude of celestial bodies:
Joyously, the moon flower is pulled along that circuitous path
Consoled that Jupiter and her moons
Will rejoin her after breaking earth's shadow.

Wailuku, 1957

Mom is ironing by the window.
It's October, the curtains hardly rustling
I watch the radio.
The pidgin announcer mangles English play by play.
The palm fronds louver a fat, Autumn moon.
In a halo, under the light pole,
The policeman drops his comics
And races to the Dairy Queen.
Earlier, some newlyweds had gone by, honking.
Mama raced to the window to yell, "Jackass!"

It's October again.
The Fall bambutcha moon crowns Haleakalā.
Stars still filter through the coconut leaves.
She's gone now,
But mama still stands by the window, ironing.

GLOSSARY AND PLACE NAMES

GLOSSARY OF HAWAIIAN WORDS

'a'ā - lava

'aha - sennit cord

A hui hou - Til we meet again

ahupua'a - land division from the mountains to the sea

'āina - land

'ākau - north

akua - God/a god

'āla'a - large tree with sap to trap birds

Ali'i Nui - Great Chief

Aloha īa 'oe - Hello/goodbye to you.

Aloha kākou - Hello/goodbye everyone including yourself.

A 'oe? - And you?

'A'ole pilikia - No problem.

'ā Pele - lava

'Auwē – Oh, dear.

E 'awīwī - Come quickly!

E hele kākou - Let's go!

E hele mai - Come!

E Nei – Here!

E 'olu 'olu 'oe – Please!

hālau (hula pā) - hulahula troupe

hale - house

haole - without breath

hau - lowland tree

heiau - place of worship

Hele ma kahi'ē - Goodnight.

hone - kiss

hukilau - fishing with a seine

huli - turn over

'ili 'ili - small, smooth shoreline rocks

I mua - Onward!

kālā - money

kalo – taro

kālua – underground cooking

kamani - large tree

kanaka maoli - original settlers of Hawai'i

kapa - tapa made from wauke for clothes/bedding

kaula 'ili - leather rope

keiki - child

kiamanu - bird catcher

kiawe - thorny tree

kīhei - shawl

ki'i - statue/image

koa - hardwood tree

kolohe - mischievous

kukui - candlewood tree

kūlolo – taro (kalo) pudding
kupuna - ancestor/grandparent
ku'uipo - sweetheart
laua'e - fern
lauhala - pandanus leaves used
for plaiting
laulau - pork cooked in ki
leaves
lava-lava (malo) - waist wrap-
around
lehua - flower of the 'ōhi'a tree
loa - large tree
lo'i - taro (kalo) patch
lōlō - crazy
Lono - Hawaiian god
lua - hole/toilet
lū'au - Hawaiian feast
mahalo - thanks
maika'i - fine/well
maka - eye(s)
makai - seaward
makapi'api'a - viscous matter
in the eyes
maka'u - scared
make - dead
mākuahine - mother
makuakāne - father
makule - old
malo - waist wrap-around
mana - power
manini - stingy amount
mauka - mountainward

ma'ukele - forest
moa - chicken
moa kāne - rooster
momona - fat
Muku - 30th Night of the
Moon (moonless)
mu'umu'u - Mother Hubbard
dress
nīele - nosey
niu - coconut tree
'ohana - family
'ōkolehao - liquor distilled
from ti (ki) root
'ōhi'a - tree with Lehua
blossoms
'opihi - limpets
'ōpū - stomach
'Ōlelo Hawai'i - Hawaiian
language
Pākē - Chinese
pala'ie - ball in the loop game
pali - cliff
pāhoehoe - smooth lava
pānini - prickly pear cactus
papa'i - crabs
pau hana - finish work
Pehea 'oe? - How are you?
pili - grass used for huts
pipi - cow
poi - Hawaiian staff of life from
kalo
poi dog - mixed breed

pouwai'ū - tying bull to tree to
tame
puka - window/door/hole
pūpū - appetizer
tūtūwahine - grandmother
uahi 'awa - smoke dust
'ulu - breadfruit

uku - payment
wai - water
wai puna - ocean underwater
spring
wahine - woman
wala'au - talk story
wa'u - scrape

PLACE NAMES

MAUI

Haleakalā - Volcano - House of
the Sun - 10,022 feet
Hāna - village in East Maui
Honua'ula - South Maui -
La Perouse Area
'Īao - valley and stream in
Central Maui
Kahakuloa - North Maui
village
Kaho'olawe - island off south
coast of Maui
Kahului - town and port in
Central Maui
Kalama Park - recreation area
in Kihei
Kama'ole - beaches of South
Maui

Kanaio - area on south slope of
Haleakalā
Kaupō - small village in East
Maui
Ke'anae - peninsular village in
East Maui
Keawakapu - beach at Mākena
(today Wailea)
Keone'ō'io Bay - known today
as La Perouse Bay
Kepaniwai - dam and area of
'Īao Stream
Kihei - village in South Maui
Kīpahulu - area between Hāna
and Kaupō
Kohemālamalama - ancient
name for Kaho'olawe
Kula - upcountry south flank
of Haleakalā

Lahaina - town and port of West Maui

Lāhainaluna - School above Lahaina Town

Māʻalaea/Kamāʻalaea - beach and harbor Central Maui

Makawao - upcountry Town on west flank of Haleakalā

Mākena - South Maui area and beaches

Mauna Kahalewai - Hawaiian name for West Maui Mountains

Mill Camp - planatation laborers' village in Wailuku

Molokini - small caldera between Maui and Kahoʻolawe

Nāhiku - small village in East Maui

Nāpili - village in West Maui

ʻOheʻo Stream and Falls - East Maui major stream and falls

Pāʻia - East Maui Village

Palihea Stream - stream in Palikū Forest Reserve

Palikū - area in Haleakalā Crater

Paukūkalo - Central Maui village

Puʻukukui - Highest peak of West Maui Mountains - 5,788 feet

Puʻuokamoa (ʻĪao Needle) - phallic formation aka Kūkaemoku - 2,250 feet

Puʻu Māhoe - area in Honuaʻula

Puʻuʻolaʻola - overlook area of Haleakalā (Red Hill)

Seven Sacred Pools - succession of pools from ʻOheʻo Falls to the ocean

ʻUlupalakua - upland, country area of Mākena

Wahikuli - area upland of Lahaina

Waiehu - ocean area in Central Maui

Waiheʻe - village in Central Maui

Wailuku - town located below West Maui Mountains/ Central Maui

ELSEWHERE IN HAWAI'I

Halemaʻumaʻu - crater within
larger Kilaueʻa Crater,
Hawaiʻi Big Island

Hawaiʻi Nui - another name
for the Big Island

Hilo - city, port, and capital of
the Big Island

Honolulu - city and port in
South Oʻahu/Hawaiʻi capital

Kāʻu – Southern Big Island
district

Puna - Southeast Big Island
district

Schofield - military barracks
on Oʻahu

Wailuku River - major stream
that runs through Hilo

BY THE SAME AUTHOR

BOOKS (Published by Punawai Press)

Under the Star of Gladness *(I Lalo o Hōkūleʻa)/ʻIliʻIli:* Two Plays, 1994.

Children of the Turning Tide/Still Born *(Na Mele O Kahoʻolawe):* Two Plays, 1999.

Hibiscus Pomade/Steamer Days/Tandy: Three Plays, 2007.

PLAYS

Still Born *(Nā Mele o Kahoʻolawe)*
History and liberation of the island of Kahoʻolawe.
Produced by Maui Community Theater, 1991.

ʻIli ʻIli
A Hawaiian entertainer and the Spirit of Charles Lindbergh team up to save Hāna from a massive development.
Produced by Maui Community Theater, 1991.

Children of the Turning Tide
Hawaiʻi's future monarchs as teens at the Royal School.
Produced by Baldwin Theater Guild, 1992.

Under the Star of Gladness *(I Lalo o Hōkūleʻa)*
Three generations of a Portuguese family and friends in Hawaiʻi.
Produced by Maui Community Theater, 1993.

People of the First Year
The first Japanese Christians on Maui.
Produced by ʻĪao Congregational Church, 1994.

Steamer Days: The View from Aloha Tower
A romantic romp through a 1938 Honolulu Boat Day with Duke
Kahanamoku, Hilo Hattie, and Shirley Temple.
Produced by Baldwin Theater Guild, 1996.

Hawaiian Kine Christmas Carol
An 1889 Sprecklesville Mill kine version of the Dickens' classic.
Produced by Maui Community Theater, 1997.

Kamapuaʻa: The Exploits of the Pig God
The demigod Kamapuaʻa raises havoc and confronts the fire
goddess Pele.
Produced by Hawaii Leadership Conference for Nā Kumu ʻŌlelo
Hawaiʻi, Maui Community College, 1997.

Pele and Hiʻiaka: Sisters of Fire
The odyssey of the Pele Family and Hiʻiaka's journey to escort
Lohiʻau from Kauaʻi to Halemaʻumaʻu,
Written 1997, to be produced.

Tandy!
The libretto of an opera based on the rise and fall of Hāna-born
opera singer, Tandy MacKenzie.
Written 2002, to be produced.

Hibiscus Pomade
'60s musical when Hawaiian music met rock 'n roll with Lucky,
Aku and the KPOI Boys.
Produced by Baldwin Theater Guild, 2004.

Only the Morning Star Knows: In Search of Kamehameha
The search for the bones of Kamehameha leads King Kalākaua into
the mind of Hawaiʻi's greatest monarch.
Written 2003, to be produced.

ʻĪao: Where We Walk Through Rainbows
The stories of the sacred valley from prehistory to modern times.
Written 2004, to be produced.

FILMS

The Chair Resistance, Producer, West Valley Productions, 1980.

Laugh Trax, Producer and Segment Director, West Valley Productions, 1981.

Standing in the Shadows, Producer, West Valley Productions, 1982.

Aloha, Sweetheart (Aloha ʻOe, E Kuʻu Ipo), Screenplay, 2008.

OTHER STORIES, POEMS, MUSIC, AND LYRICS

"Kepaniwai" (Short Story), in *University of Dayton Literary Journal,* 1969. On display at the Pacific Tsunami Museum, Hilo.

"Maui Moon Blues" (Music and Lyrics), from the drama, Still Born *(Nā Mele o Kahoʻolawe),* 1983.

"The Makawao Fourth of July Parade" (Music and Lyrics), 2000.

"Hibiscus Pomade" (Music and Lyrics), from the musical comedy, Hibiscus Pomade, 2002.

"More Hibiscus Pomade" (Music and Lyrics), from the musical comedy sequel, Hibiscus Pomade 2. 2004.

"Ke One o Ka Puʻu Hale Nani" (Lyrics), Music by Pekelo Cosma, 2008.

ABOUT THE ARTIST

David Sandell has been living on Maui for forty years and has drawn virtually every dilapidated street, intriguing café, and historic site he has crossed, spinning out massive silk screens and murals along the way, his bold illustrations appearing in numerous newspapers and magazines.

He lives with his wife Virginia, an actress, director, and drama instructor, in an old cane house in Wailuku Town, nestled in the opening shadows of mystical ʻĪao Valley. He rarely ventures farther than his art gallery on Market Street, where he says he "promotes the loftier slumming persona of a topical cartoonist."

koa books

Koa Books publishes works on Hawaiian culture, current affairs, and personal transformation. Please visit www.koabooks.com for a list of recent and forthcoming books.

Koa Books
PO Box 822
Kihei, Hawai'i 96753
www.koabooks.com